A SHARP GRATING OF METAL ON METAL BROKE THE SILENCE. . . .

Instinctively Foxx glanced at the door leading to the corridor. He stepped to the dresser and was picking up the Cloverleaf revolver when the door between his room and Maxine's swung open.

Maxine stood there, her hair unbound and cascading over her shoulders. The light from her room streamed through the almost transparent fabric of her nightgown and silhouetted the contours of her body.

"I thought," she said, stopped, and started over. "I wanted— Well, it's been such a lovely evening, Foxx, that I just hated to see it end. . . ."

FOXX'S FOE

Zack Tyler

A DELL BOOK

Published by
Dell Publishing Co., Inc.
1 Dag Hammarskjold Plaza
New York, New York 10017

ISBN: 0-440-12526-X

Printed in the United States of America
First printing—September 1982

CHAPTER 1

Giving the neck of the champagne bottle a final twirl, the waiter at the Cliff House lifted his hands with a flourish to indicate that the wine was chilled. He pulled the green bottle out of the ice-bucket, rested it on a snow-white napkin, and held it up so Foxx could see the label.

Foxx nodded. He and Vida Martin had come from San Francisco for dinner at the famous oceanside restaurant, a habit they'd formed early in their relationship. Whenever Foxx was leaving on a case, they'd have dinner at the Cliff House the evening before he left.

In the afterglow of their meal they'd been sitting in silence, gazing across the gently rolling surface of the Pacific Ocean at the setting sun, which was gilding the tops of the low waves. Now they watched as their waiter wrapped the napkin around the bottle, stripped the gold foil off the neck, removed the wire cage, and worked the cork out carefully until it came free with a gentle pop.

Vida and Foxx sat facing each other across their round table. The waiter poured the bubbling amber wine and returned the bottle to the ice-bucket before bowing and withdrawing.

"I love to see champagne served," Vida smiled.

Lifting her glass, she added, "Almost as much as I enjoy drinking it."

"Most ladies do," Foxx said. He raised his glass.

Both of them were leaning forward across the table, their arms extended in a toast, when the sharp crack of a rifle rang out and the large plate-glass window next to their table shattered, cascading in jagged chunks to the floor.

Foxx reacted instantly. With his free hand he upended the table, and grasping Vida's wrist, he quickly pulled her behind its shelter.

Around them the other Cliff House patrons were scrambling for cover. A second rifleshot cracked from outside the restaurant, cutting through the high shrill cries of women and the angry rumble of men's voices inside. The second slug slammed into the thick tabletop, passed through it, and dropped harmlessly to the floor between Vida and Foxx, who were still crouched behind the table.

Foxx paid no attention to the shiny chunk of lead or to the melee inside the restaurant. He was peering around the rim of the table, his keen eyes searching the ragged gray cliffs that rose abruptly in a wide arc above the narrow strip of sandy beach that began near the restaurant, a beach made narrower now by the incoming tide.

"Do you see anything?" Vida asked, her voice strained but steady.

"I got enough of a look at that last shot to see where whoever's doing the shooting is holed up." Foxx put a hand on Vida's shoulder and went on, "You stay right here and you'll be safe. Just don't stand up or try to look outside."

"What're you going to do?" Vida asked.

Foxx was sitting on his heels, peering intently

through the shattered window. He did not take his eyes off the spot where he'd seen the dark wisp of muzzle smoke rise against pink sky.

"I'm going after him," he replied.

Vida started to speak, but changed her mind. Hearing the anger in Foxx's voice, she realized there was no point in trying to persuade him not to go.

"There's not much of a place where the bastard can hole up," Foxx went on. "There's no cover on those cliffs, and nothing but bare sand between them and the water. I've just got to get closer to him. All I've got's my Cloverleaf Colt, and those cliffs are well out of its range."

Vida nodded. She didn't waste breath cautioning Foxx to be careful. She watched while he rose and, still crouching, began running toward the door of the restaurant.

A plank walkway fifteen or twenty feet long, with a waist-high railing, bridged the isolated rock formation on which the Cliff House stood and the main bluffs that lined the Pacific shore on the San Francisco peninsula.

Foxx ran at a crouch across the bridge, getting what protection he could from the high railing. He kept his mind fixed on the image of the jutting stone pillar from which the sniper had fired, and when he reached the end of the walkway, he stopped and peered around the last posts of the railing to get his bearings.

He was a good hundred yards from the cliff where he'd seen the wisp of gunsmoke. At that late afternoon hour on a chilly day, the beachfront was deserted except for three or four livery hacks that stood across the broad sandy roadway from the restaurant. The drivers were sitting in one of the carriages, chatting. Apparently none of them had heard the shooting, which was not surprising because a stiff breeze was blowing across the peninsula from the bay and would have carried the sounds with it.

Foxx swore silently at Junius Foster for having built his restaurant in such an isolated spot, picturesque though it might be. To reach the sniper, Foxx was going to have to make his way across ground that offered no concealment at all.

Where the Cliff House stood, the tall dark-gray bluffs that lined the shore for a mile or so jutted right out to the waters of the Pacific Ocean. The restaurant itself had been built on a huge stone formation separated from the main cliffs by a wide, deep fissure. The bluff on which the building stood rose almost vertically from the water itself, so that even at low tide there was barely room to walk between the base of the massive rock and the ocean.

A short distance to the north of the restaurant the cliffs dropped straight into the sea. To the south the narrow strip of sandy beach, not more than a half mile or so in length, ran between the base of the cliffs and the water's edge. At high tide the strip of sand was reduced to a width of only a few yards. It was on the top of one of the fingerlike cliffs that jutted irregularly toward the water that Foxx had seen the thread of gunsmoke.

"Now, whoever that son of a bitch is, he ain't going to get no closer to the Cliff House," Foxx muttered to himself as he checked the terrain. "And if he scouted this place at all, he'll know there ain't no way to go but south."

Foxx stood up, gambling on drawing the sniper's fire if the man still lurked on top of the cliffs, waiting for a second chance. No shot broke the low whistle of the wind, and no sign of life could be seen on the cliffs.

Foxx started at a slow run toward the cliffs just south of the spot where the shots had come from.

As he moved, his eyes scanning the tops of the cliffs for any sign of the sniper's presence, he drew his Cloverleaf Colt from the pouch-holster sewn into the lining of his coat behind the lapel.

Without taking his eyes off the terrain before him, Foxx thumbed the hammer back to full cock. The hammer's movement ratcheted the four-chamber cylinder a half-turn to place a shell in firing position. He knew the little revolver wouldn't be effective at the distance that still remained, but he counted on a snap shot discouraging the sniper.

Foxx had covered half the distance to the cliffs before he got a glimpse of the man who had tried to kill him. Even then it was only a flash of movement, the edge of a man's arm as he raised it, shifting position on the rim of the cliff. Foxx dropped flat on the ground and began crawling forward. The sun had dropped out of sight now below the ocean's rim, but its afterglow was still bright enough to force him to squint.

He'd crawled twenty or thirty feet when he got a good look at his quarry. This time the sniper rose to his knees, his eyes fixed on the Cliff House. Foxx froze, his dark suit merging with the deep gray rock forming the top of the cliff.

He could see the sniper clearly now, but only in silhouette against the still-bright sky. The man was kneeling, one hand gripping the barrel of his rifle, the butt of the weapon resting on the flat rock where he knelt. He was gazing intently at the Cliff House.

Foxx glanced in that same direction. Inside the restaurant he could see figures moving, but lying flat on the ground as he was, he could make out no detail. Foxx knew that the man on the cliff could get a better view from his position, which took advantage of the broad windows that formed three walls of the restaurant.

Instinct more than anything else warned Foxx when the sniper saw him. The kneeling man dropped flat. As he moved he swung his rifle up and fired. Foxx had rolled aside the instant he'd realized he'd been seen. The rifle slug scored the hard rock of the cliff where Foxx had been lying and ricocheted off in the direction of the low-growing junipers and salt cedars that dotted the sand dunes stretching inland from the top of the cliff.

Foxx immediately sprang up, crouched low, and ran toward the sniper, gambling that he could cover a few yards while his assailant was levering a fresh shell into the chamber of his rifle. He dove flat a split second before another shot whistled over his head.

His dash had brought Foxx close enough for the Cloverleaf Colt to be effective, but he did not return the sniper's fire. The revolver held only four shells, and he had no intention of wasting a shot without a target.

Foxx wriggled forward, close to the edge of the cliff, but he saw no sign of the sniper. He reached the rim of the rough gray stone and looked down. The sniper had slung his rifle muzzle-down across his back in order to use both hands while he climbed down, bracing himself in a narrow fissure that broke the sheer stone face of the cliff.

Now Foxx fired. The sniper moved in the split second that Foxx's finger tightened on the Colt's trigger, but the slug from the wicked little .44-caliber Cloverleaf smashed into the butt of the rifle, dislodging the man from his precarious position.

He began sliding down the cleft in the cliff's face, scrabbling in vain at the rock's surface as he tried to find a handhold. The cliff was fifty or sixty feet high at the summit, and the sniper had covered a bit more than half the distance before Foxx's shot had forced him to lose his balance. The sniper fought to stop his slide, but he'd gained too much momentum. His efforts jarred free his rifle, which flew through the air and landed in the sand at the base of the bluff. Seconds later the man himself hit the sand at the bottom of the cliff with a muffled thud, and lay still.

Foxx watched him for a moment, and when the man did not move but remained lying facedown on the sandy beach, Foxx slid his revolver back into its holster and started down himself. The descent was not as difficult as he'd thought. Foxx found that he could brace his feet on either side of the cleft and that the fissure was wide enough to allow him to keep himself balanced upright.

Still, climbing down required Foxx's full attention, so he did not notice when the sniper first got to his feet. The unknown attacker had already gained a substantial lead by the time Foxx looked down and saw him running along the narrow strip of beach. Foxx dropped the last fifteen feet to the sand and, drawing his Colt again, started running after the fleeing man.

Underfoot, the sand was soft and shifting and Foxx could gain no ground on the sniper, who was already dodging along the base of the cliffs, which curved toward the water's edge as the strip of beach grew narrower.

Foxx still did not shoot. Daylight was fading fast, and shooting on the run was a chancy business under the best conditions. Foxx did not want to risk a running snap shot that might kill his quarry. He wanted the man alive, wanted to find out who he was and why he'd made his attack.

He redoubled his efforts, but the fleeing man was a good fifty yards ahead of Foxx when the cliffs suddenly slanted down to disappear under the sand of the beach. When Foxx rounded the end of the cliffs, there was no sign of the sniper in front of him. All he could see across the wide sandy road were the dark humps of scrub cedar and juniper bushes growing thickly on the sand dunes that he knew stretched for almost a mile from the beach. The juniper grew low to the soil, seldom more than knee-high, but the salt cedars were as tall as a man's shoulders. In the quick-settling darkness they would effectively hide a fugitive from searchers an arm's length away. Foxx crossed the road, stepped behind a cedar, and took out one of the twisted Italian fisherman's stogies he favored. As he lit it he considered his situation.

An army would be required to search the brushy area into which the sniper had disappeared, and though Foxx could summon several dozen railroad police and detectives, it would take time. During the two hours required to gather a search party, the sniper would certainly vanish.

Taking an angry drag on his stogie, Foxx turned away and started back toward the beach where the sniper had left his rifle lying at the foot of the cliff. Perhaps the gun would give him a clue as to the unknown's identity.

By the time Foxx had retrieved the rifle, its stock badly splintered where the slug from the Colt had struck it, darkness had settled over the beach. He trudged across the sand, backtracking around the end of the cliffs, and walked along the road back to the Cliff House.

Vida Martin was staring anxiously at the door when Foxx entered the restaurant. Her frown turned into a smile of relief when she saw him. Foxx walked over to the table.

"I don't suppose I need to tell you how much better I feel, now that you're back safely," she said, her voice barely more than a whisper.

"That shooting didn't amount to much," Foxx told her, pulling out a chair and sitting down. He laid the rifle on the floor beside his chair.

"But—you've got his gun."

"I don't get a lot of credit for that," Foxx said, lighting a fresh stogie. "Whoever it was, he missed me twice and I missed him once. He dropped the rifle while he was climbing down the cliffs. I never was close enough to get a good look at him, dark as it was getting."

Junius Foster came hurrying up to the table. The Cliff House owner's ruddy face was twisted into a worried frown. He said, "I do hope you're not hurt, Mr. Foxx."

"Oh, I'm all right. Just some harebrained lunatic decided to take a potshot at me. That's part of my job, I guess."

"I can't tell you how much I regret what happened, Mr. Foxx," Foster said. "To think that my establishment should be the scene of such an affair! Perhaps we need to reorganize the Committee of Vigilance again!"

"Not likely," Foxx replied. "Whoever took them shots didn't have a thing to do with any gang, at least not any San Francisco gang. Like I said, it's part of my job. Chances are it was somebody taking out a grudge against the C&K, somebody I nabbed and sent up to the pen."

Foster shook his head. "I still regret it, Mr. Foxx. You're the guest of the house for dinner, of course, and a fresh bottle of champagne is on its way up from the cellar right now."

"That's a nice thing for you to do, Junius, and I appreciate it. But I think me and Vida both need something a little bit stronger than champagne."

"Of course!" Foster said. "I'll tell the maître d' to save the champagne for your next visit, and have a bottle of Cyrus Noble sent over from the bar."

"And some fresh coffee, if you don't mind, Mr. Foster," Vida put in.

Foxx looked around the restaurant while they waited for the whiskey and coffee to arrive. Tablecloths had been tacked up to cover the window broken by the rifle shots. The tables and chairs that had been upset when their occupants began milling around had been righted and reset. Only two of the other tables were still occupied; apparently most of the diners had left abruptly after the first flurry of excitement following the shooting.

"Do you really think it's safe to stay here?" Vida frowned. She looked around the big room. "All those windows—"

"Vida," Foxx said gently, "whoever took those shots is long gone. Anyhow, I got his rifle. He ain't apt to come close enough to use a pistol, after the chase I gave him."

"I suppose you're right," she nodded. Then, with a half smile, she added, "I'm not sure I want to risk what reputation I have left by being seen with you. You look like a hobo who's just hopped off a C&K freight after a long, hard trip."

For the first time, Foxx looked at his clothing. The knees of his carefully tailored trousers were shredded and yellow from the sand that still clung to them. His patent leather boots, made by Ffoulkes & Bradley in London, were scuffed, and in several places deep white scars marred their black gloss. There was a rip in the lapel of his coat where it had been snagged on the rough stone of the cliff as he climbed down in pursuit of the sniper. His hands were grimy, and a few scratches showed red through the layer of dirt.

"Well, you and me both know that I got a change of clothes back at my place," he smiled. "And I guess that's all that counts. But it'd be a good idea for me to go wash up while we're waiting for the coffee to get here."

As they sat sipping their coffee a few moments later, Vida asked Foxx, "Do you have any idea why this man would want to kill you?"

"Not a glimmer. Like I told Junius Foster, it could be anybody that's carrying a grudge against me or the C&K."

"Which takes in a lot of territory," she said thoughtfully.

"It does," Foxx agreed. "That rifle I picked up after he got away might give me a lead, though. I'll look into that first thing tomorrow morning."

"I thought you were leaving to handle that new case tomorrow."

"That's how it was supposed to be. Jim Flaherty was dead set on me getting out there as soon as possible. But he'll just have to put up with me leaving a day later'n I figured. If that gun is going to give me a lead, I've got to follow it up before it gets cold. If I put it off till I come back, whoever I'm looking for will sure as hell be long gone."

"How long will you be able to stay in San Francisco?"

"Now, that's something I can't say, Vida," he answered with a thoughtful frown. "I've got to run the sniper down right quick or Jim's going to get pretty riled up at me. But he won't fuss too much if I just take a day or two."

"Then we'll have dinner here again before you leave?"

"Why, sure. You ought to've known that."

"Good."

Foxx refilled their glasses. "You'd rather be traveling with me on my cases, wouldn't you?" he asked her.

"Yes. I might not be much help, but at least we'd be together. I'm afraid I'm not the kind of woman who can kiss my man good-bye and then quietly knit while I wait for him to come back."

"That's never bothered you before."

"I know," she shrugged. "I guess being shot at by that sniper's bothering me more than I realized."

Foxx sat in silence for a moment, looking across the table at Vida. She was a beautiful woman, with her deep auburn hair set off by flawless skin and dark flashing eyes.

There was only one barrier between them, if it could be called that. Vida's sister was the wife of Caleb Petersen, president of the California & Kansas Railroad, and Foxx was the chief of the road's detective division.

He and Vida had agreed in the beginning that to avoid family complications, she and Foxx would keep their relationship private and do nothing to draw attention to their long-standing affair. They'd also agreed that there'd be no questions asked about their conduct while they were apart. So far, the agreement had been kept, and Foxx hoped it would continue that way.

Now he asked Vida, "You're sure it ain't more than just the sniper that's bothering you?"

She looked levelly at him for a moment, and nodded. "Yes. I'm sure. And if you've finished your coffee, why don't we go? I can always brew a pot when we get to my flat."

"That's a right smart idea," Foxx agreed.

He caught the eye of the waiter who'd served them, and gestured for the man to bring the check. Junius Foster must have been watching, for instead of the waiter it was the proprietor who came to the table.

"There is no check, Mr. Foxx," he said. "You are my guest, as I told you. And I hope tonight's unfortunate affair won't cause you to desert the Cliff House."

"Don't worry," Foxx assured him. "Me and Vida will likely be back tomorrow or the next day."

"We'll be ready to serve you," Foster said, walking beside them to the door.

Once they were inside the hackney cab that had been waiting for them, Vida took Foxx's hand and said, "Don't take me too seriously. I'm as satisfied as you are with our arrangement. I don't *really* sit home and knit when you're away from San Francisco, you know."

"Sure. I wouldn't want you to, either. You know that."

"I know," she nodded.

Suddenly Vida smiled, and Foxx could see that whatever had been weighing on her mind was gone. He leaned toward her and she brought up her lips to meet his. They clung together for a moment, Vida's tongue seeking out Foxx's, caressing it, while her hand crept to his thigh and stroked him gently.

"It's a long way to town, Foxx," she whispered when their lips finally parted. "And I don't feel like waiting until we get to my flat."

CHAPTER 2

Foxx could barely see Vida's face in the cab's dark interior, but the urgency in her voice told him all he needed to know. The hackney was a double-seater, narrow but long. The hackman's seat was high, and the only way he could communicate with his passengers was through a hatch in the roof of the carriage. Foxx glanced outside; the road from the ocean to San Francisco was unlit; the carriage lamps on each side of the hackman's seat provided barely enough illumination for the driver to see ahead.

"I'm as ready as you are," Foxx told Vida. "And I'd say this is about as private a place as we could hope to find."

Vida was already busy unbuttoning his fly, sliding her hand inside his drawers to free Foxx's straining manhood.

Foxx lifted her skirt and petticoats and found the waistband of her pantalettes. He fumbled at the buttons until he got the waistband open, and Vida arched her back, lifting herself off the seat to let Foxx pull the pantalettes off. His fingers slid over the smooth skin of her stomach and down to the curly warmth between her legs.

Without interrupting her attention to Foxx's throb-

bing penis, Vida parted her legs. She gasped as Foxx's
fingers entered her moist opening.

"You were so brave," she whispered to Foxx, her
breath warm on his ear. "And I'm so happy that you
came back safely—to me."

Vida bent down and Foxx felt her warm mouth
close over him, her tongue moving softly against the
sensitive tip of his erection. She opened her thighs to
let his fingers penetrate deeper. The delicate folds
quivered when he rubbed them softly before slipping
his fingers into the even warmer depths that Vida
opened for him.

Foxx hardened under the urgent caresses of Vida's
lips and tongue until he could stand it no longer, and
when she released him and straightened up, he lifted
her bodily from the hackney's seat while he moved under her.

Vida spread her legs to straddle Foxx's hips with her
thighs. He felt her hand guide him into her, and then
he slowly eased her down. Vida groaned ecstatically.

"Oh, lovely!" she gasped, a rippling shudder seizing
her as she pressed to meet Foxx's upthrust groin.
"Hold me a minute, Foxx! I don't want to let go yet,
but I can't control myself."

Foxx stayed motionless, his strong hands easily sup-
porting Vida above him. Her shudders continued for a
few moments and then she sighed softly.

"Now," she said.

Foxx thrust upward and a small cry of pleasure
burst from Vida's lips. She pushed down to meet his
hips each time they rose. Then she began trembling
and moaning softly. Foxx brought his hips up harder
and increased the tempo until Vida tensed and her
moans grew into an ecstatic cry. Foxx did not hold

back but exploded as Vida's convulsive shudders ended
and she slumped forward on him, inert and exhausted.

For several minutes the only sound inside the hackney was the grating of its wheels on the graveled roadway. Finally Vida stirred and raised her head from
Foxx's shoulder.

"I'd love an encore," she said, "but I don't think we
have time. We must almost be to town by now." She
twisted around to peer out the small high window set
in the hackney's door. "I can see lights ahead."

"Don't worry about encores," Foxx said. "The
night's still young."

Vida lifted herself from Foxx's hips and began rear-
ranging her skirts. "I feel like a scarlet woman, Foxx,"
she chuckled; "I've always wanted to make love in a
cab, but this is the first time I've had the chance."

"I sorta liked it myself," Foxx told her. "Even if it
ain't quite as comfortable as a bed."

"A few minutes more and you can be as comfortable
as you like. That is, if you're still in the mood."

"Now, that's something you don't have to worry
about," Foxx said. "As long as it's you I'm with, I
don't care whether it's a hired hack, a bed, or a barn."

Foxx lighted one of his twisted stogies, and they sat
in fulfilled silence while the hackney rumbled on to
stop in front of Vida's flat, on Pine Street near Larkin.
Foxx slipped a quarter-eagle into the hackie's hand before getting out of the cab, and took Vida's arm as
they walked to the door of the building in which her
flat occupied half of the second floor. She had her key
ready, and they were upstairs and in the cozy parlor of
the flat almost before the rattling of the hackney's
wheels on the brick pavement had died away.

Vida had left a lamp on the table, its wick turned

low. She turned the wick up to brighten the lamp's light, and looked at Foxx over her shoulder.

"You do look terrible, you know," she said. "Would you like me to draw a tub of hot water for you to bathe in?"

Foxx smiled and said, "Only if you'll keep me company."

Turning to Foxx, Vida said, "My tub's not as big as the one you have at the Cosmopolitan, of course—"

"Somehow we'll find a way to fit into it," Foxx told her.

He held out his arms and Vida moved into his embrace. Their lips clung in a prolonged kiss that left them both breathless. Vida's hand crept down to the bulge in Foxx's pants and caressed him gently. "Let's undress in the bedroom while the tub's filling."

Foxx took his Cloverleaf Colt out of its pouch-holster and laid it on Vida's dressing table before letting the coat drop to the chair that stood in front of the table. He heard the water start running in the adjoining bathroom and began levering off his boots. As he stood in front of the dressing table taking off his cravat, Vida came back into the room.

"I'm glad it's only your clothes that were hurt," she said as she came up to Foxx and turned her back so that he could undo the long row of buttons that ran up the back of her shirtwaist. "You can always buy new ones. And you've certainly got enough boots so that you won't miss one pair."

"Oh, I'll write to Ffoulkes soon as I get a chance and tell him to make me up another pair of patent leathers," Foxx said, holding Vida's arm while she stepped out of the skirt she'd unfastened and let it drop to the floor.

She shrugged out of her camisole, and Foxx was

struck—as he always was—by the beauty of her full,
firmly rounded breasts; Vida arched her back as Foxx's
lips moved slowly over them. Under his tongue Foxx
felt her nipples swell and grow firm as he continued to
caress them.

Vida was twisting in his arms now, her skin soft under his hands as he rubbed his palms over her smooth
shoulders and down her back. Vida unbuttoned the
waistband of her petticoat and let the garment slide to
the floor. She hadn't put her pantalettes back on, so
she stood before him naked now. Foxx drew back and
looked at her.

"You better turn off that bathtub," he told her. "I
got a feeling it'll be a while before we're ready for it."

An hour later they still had not bathed. They were
lying side by side on Vida's wide bed, her head resting
comfortably on Foxx's broad shoulder, both of them
feeling pleasantly exhausted, when the clanging of the
doorbell broke the silence. Vida jumped up with a start
and looked at Foxx with a puzzled frown.

"I can't think of anyone who'd be ringing my doorbell at this time of the night, Foxx. Did you leave word
at the C&K office that you'd be here?"

"You know I wouldn't do a fool thing like that,
Vida."

"I don't think I'll answer the door, then," Vida told
him. "It might just be someone ringing my bell by mistake."

The bell clanged again, this time more urgently. It
still had not stopped when Foxx rolled off the bed and
picked up his trousers.

"Whoever it is ain't giving up," he said. "You mind
if I go down and see who it is?"

"Wait just a minute while I slip on a robe and get
my keys. I'd better go with you, in case it's Clara or

Caleb, though why they'd be ringing my bell at this time of night is more than I can imagine."

Foxx picked up the Colt from the dressing table, then as an afterthought put it down and slid his arms into the sleeves of his shirt. He said, "If it's someone we know, I'd better look halfway dressed."

The doorbell stopped ringing as suddenly as it had begun. In the silence Foxx and Vida stood for a moment, looking at each other.

"It sounds like whoever was ringing has given up," Vida said in a half whisper.

"Or they're just waiting a minute before they try again," Foxx said. "We better go have a look, just in case."

As they started down the stairway Vida frowned thoughtfully and remarked, "I'm sure Clara knows you and I are seeing each other when you're in San Francisco. And if she knows, I imagine Caleb does too. But neither of them has said anything to me."

"No reason why they should," Foxx told her. "You're a grown-up woman, you can do whatever you please."

"But Clara can't forget she's my big sister. She tries not to let it show, but I know she feels responsible for me."

When they reached the first-floor hallway the hall was dark, but the gas streetlight across the way shone through the small pane of glass inset at eye-level in the entry door. Foxx kept to one side of the peephole as he went to the door and looked through the small high pane.

"Whoever was ringing, they've gone," he told Vida over his shoulder.

"Are you sure?"

"Sure as can be, for all I can see through this

peephole." Holding the Cloverleaf Colt ready, Foxx opened the door a crack and peered out. "There's nobody out there."

Vida came up to stand behind him. "Let's step out to the sidewalk and see if anyone's on the street," she suggested.

When they reached the bottom of the entryway and looked along Pine Street, there were no pedestrians on the sidewalk, no carriages in the street.

"Must've been a drunk, ringing the wrong bell," Foxx said. "Or somebody who thinks it's funny to go around rousing folks in the middle of the night."

"I suppose so," Vida nodded. "We might as well go back upstairs and have that bath."

Foxx was pushing the front door open when Vida called him, her voice sharp and puzzled.

"Foxx. Am I seeing things, or is there a letter in my mailbox?" she asked.

Foxx stepped back to look and saw the unmistakable gleam of white paper behind the metal grill of the mailbox door.

"It's a letter, all right," he said.

"That's impossible," Vida replied. "I took in the afternoon mail before we went to the Cliff House, and I know I glanced at the mailbox door when we came in. I always do, it's a habit."

"You must've missed it, then."

"That's impossible!" Vida's voice was positive. "How could I have missed it then and see it now? Whoever was ringing my doorbell must have put that letter in my box."

"Well, let's go take a look," Foxx suggested.

They went into the foyer and Vida unlocked the mailbox.

"It's not a letter," she said, as she took the paper

from the box. "Just a note of some kind, folded up." She held the paper up to the light that spilled in through the peephole. "I can't read it here, the light's too dim. Let's go upstairs so I can see what it says."

In Vida's flat, Foxx stood waiting while she read the note. He saw her eyes widen, her full lips open. She looked up from the note, and stared unseeingly at Foxx. Then she handed him the paper.

Foxx read the message quickly. There were only a few lines, scrawled in pencil on coarse ruled paper such as might have come from a child's school tablet. The message was in the large formless hand of one unaccustomed to writing.

"Vida Martin," the note said, "yore luck was in tonite and mine wasent. I misset you and that Foxx sunabitch this time but nex time you can bet my aims gone to be better."

For a long moment, both Foxx and Vida were silent. Then she asked in a small worried voice, "Whoever wrote this was certainly no scholar, but he got his message across. Did it occur to you, out at the Cliff House, that the sniper was aiming at me too, Foxx?"

Foxx took his time replying. At last he said, "I guess that's about the last thing I'd've thought of, Vida, although that note doesn't leave much room for doubt."

"Why me, though, Foxx?"

"It's the kind of revenge some Indians take, Vida. A Kiowa or Apache with a grudge against a man will kill one of his kinfolks or one of his clan if he can't get the man he's after."

"He must hate you a lot."

"I reckon. Whoever it is, he knows we go around together when I'm in the city. He ain't found out yet that I've got no kith or kin, and nobody much I see, except you."

"You think he means it, then?"

"He means it, sure as God made little green apples. I don't doubt that for a minute."

"But why? Who is he?"

"That's what I'd give one whole hell of a lot to know, Vida. There's a lot of men, twenty or thirty, I'd guess, that I've had a hand in putting behind bars. There's others I've crossed too. One of 'em has set out to get his revenge."

"But—" Vida stopped short. "Pour us a strong drink, Foxx. Maybe it'll wake me up enough so that I can understand all this."

Foxx took glasses and the soda siphon and a bottle of Cyrus Noble out of the liquor cabinet that stood in one corner of the room and set them on the low table between the fireplace and the divan where Vida had sat down.

He mixed a highball, half bourbon and half soda, for Vida, and poured himself a generous measure of bourbon into a smaller glass. When he moved to light a cigar, he realized that his vest and stogies were in the bedroom. He went to the bedroom and returned with a handful of the stubby twisted cigars he favored and lit one. Vida swallowed from her glass before she turned to look at him.

"You always make light of the risks you run in your job," she told Foxx soberly. "I didn't realize until tonight that I was going to be facing the same kind of risk."

"I never figured my job would rub off on you this way," Foxx told her, keeping his voice even. "I guess I should have, because some of the men I've put in prison are the kind of scum that'd think up a scheme like this."

"I guess the only time I've gotten close enough to

understand how bad some of them are was when that gang of Apaches you were after over in Arizona Territory shot up Caleb's private car." She took another sip of her drink and went on. "At least they came out in the open. The man who wrote that note shoots from ambush."

"He won't be around to worry you for long, Vida," Foxx promised. "I'll send off some wires in the morning and find out who's been let out of prison in the past few months. That might give me some idea where to start looking."

"You don't think it had anything to do with this new case?"

"It ain't real likely. The people I'll be going after this time wouldn't have got any idea I'll be trying to run 'em down. No, it's somebody from an old case that's still carrying a grudge."

"What *is* your new case, Foxx?" Vida asked.

"Train wreckers," Foxx replied. "Up in Idaho Territory."

"You mean people are deliberately wrecking C&K trains? Why? Because they're angry with the railroad?"

Foxx shook his head. "I don't think so." He thought back to his conversation with Jim Flaherty a few days earlier. "It looks to me like the C&K's just got itself caught in the middle of a mining feud."

"But—what can you do about something like that?"

"Stop it," Foxx said succinctly. Leaning forward, he tossed the butt of his stogie into the fireplace and immediately lit another. Then he went on, "Stop it, just like I'm going to stop this bastard who's trying to hurt me by hurting you."

"You don't even know who he is, Foxx. How can you stop him if you don't know where to look for him?"

"It's my business to find out things like that," Foxx reminded her. "Now, suppose you stop worrying about it, and leave that part of the job to me."

"How can I stop worrying, Foxx? Never knowing when a bullet might come out of nowhere and kill me—or you?"

"I'll figure out a way to keep you from getting hurt, Vida," Foxx promised, wondering how he was going to keep his promise. "That's part of my job too."

"And I know you're good at your job," she said. "But until you've found out who's making these threats, what do you expect me to do? Stay in this flat day and night? And what happens if he comes here after me?"

"You just put worries like that outa your mind, Vida. It's my job to see you're kept safe."

Her voice sharp, Vida asked, "Meaning that I can't look out for myself, Foxx?"

"No. Just meaning that you ain't used to handling killers. I am. That makes it my job, whether you like it or not."

Vida sat in silence for a moment, then said softly, "I'm sorry, Foxx. You're right, of course. But what will you do?"

"First thing in the morning I'll get a man here to guard the door downstairs. Don't worry about him getting in your way, you won't even know he's around."

"And then?"

"Then I'll get Jim Flaherty to put off sending me out on this new case until I've cleared up the mess I got you into. That means catching whoever is responsible and putting him behind bars again. Once that's done, it'll all be over."

"How long will it take?"

"I wish I knew. But I'll put in whatever time it

takes." When Vida made no response, Foxx went on, "It seems to me the best thing for us both to do is forget about whoever wrote that note. He sure ain't going to bother you tonight, Vida, as long as I'm with you."

"You being with me at the Cliff House didn't keep him from bothering me."

"But now we'll be on our guard, and he knows it," Foxx reminded her.

"I didn't enjoy that," Vida told him with a strained little smile. "If you want to know the truth, I was scared half to death, even if I did try not to show it."

"I never would've guessed you was scared," Foxx said truthfully. "I was real proud of you out there at the Cliff House. I still am proud of you, Vida, in every way."

This time Vida's smile was easier. "I'll do whatever you say, Foxx. I know none of this is your fault."

"It's nobody's fault except the man that's behind it." Foxx thought for a moment, then said, "Now, I'm going to stay here with you till morning. It'll be just a little bit different from what we had in mind. I'll sit up in the parlor so you can sleep without a worry in the world. Now finish filling the tub, take a good hot bath, and go to bed."

"And what will you be doing?"

"I'm going to sit right here and think."

Vida leaned toward Foxx and kissed him lightly, and in a moment Foxx heard the sound of water gushing from the bathtub faucet. He poured himself a fresh tot of Cyrus Noble and leaned back in his chair. He'd just begun to organize his thoughts when Vida called to him.

"Foxx. Come here a minute, will you?"

When Foxx reached the bathroom door, he found Vida in the tub. The clear water rippled invitingly over her creamy skin as she smiled up at him. Foxx's eyes moved from her smiling face down to her full pink-tipped breasts and on to the triangle of auburn curls between her thighs.

"What'd you want?" he asked.

"I've been doing a little thinking myself," she said. "There's not going to be anyone bothering us for the rest of the night. I don't see any reason why we should change our plans because some nut wrote me a nasty note."

"That wasn't the way you felt a few minutes ago."

"I let myself get panicked. For now I'm going to forget about that note and everything connected with it. Come on and get in here with me, Foxx. Whatever you were pondering can wait until morning."

CHAPTER 3

Foxx slipped quietly out of bed just before daybreak, leaving Vida sleeping peacefully, the deep sleep that follows total sexual exhaustion. While he dressed, Foxx decided that it would be safe to leave Vida unguarded in the flat for a few hours. The killer would be unlikely to strike during daylight hours in a busy part of town.

Carrying the rifle he'd picked up after the sniper had abandoned it, Foxx locked the door of the flat behind him and went down the steps to the street. As sunrise paled the sky he walked briskly along Pine Street until he saw a vacant hack. He hailed it, rode the rest of the way down Pine to Sansome Street, and walked the short block south on Sansome to the Cosmopolitan Hotel, his San Francisco home.

As a permanent resident of the Cosmopolitan, Foxx had come to enjoy certain privileges that the hotel did not grant its transient guests. He made his way across the deserted lobby to the main banquet hall, and then went down the service corridor to the kitchen, where he'd learned that the work of cleaning up the huge area began shortly after midnight and ended only when the famed head chef, Archille Bonaventure, began to prepare food for the day.

Foxx began looking for Archille, and finally discovered the chubby *chef de cuisine,* wearing a derby instead of his high white cap, standing outside the kitchen's alley entrance. Archille was supervising a pair of apprentices who were unloading the handcart they'd wheeled back to the hotel after having spent the hours since three o'clock accompanying Archille on his morning tour of the produce district near the waterfront.

"Foxx!" Archille greeted him. He nodded at the rifle in Foxx's hand and asked, "You are off on a hunting trip?"

"I guess you'd call it that," Foxx replied. "But it ain't the kind of trip you got in mind, I'd bet."

"N'importe," Archille shrugged. "Since you have come to look for me, I am sure you must be hungry, no?"

"I'm hungry as a bear, yes," Foxx replied. "If you'd open your restaurant at a decent hour, I wouldn't have to come back here to the kitchen now and then to beg a handout from you."

"Have I ever failed to feed you, my friend?" Archille asked, and without waiting for Foxx to answer, went on, "I am getting ready to make my own breakfast. If you will be satisfied with *œufs au beurre noir,* I will add three to the pan for you."

"That's the eggs with vinegar sauce?" Foxx asked. Archille nodded, and Foxx added, "They tasted pretty good last time you made some for me."

"Eh bien," Archille smiled. "We breakfast together, then, *mon ami.*"

With three of the richly smothered eggs, several slices of crisp toast, and two cups of steaming black coffee under his belt, Foxx's spirits improved tremendously. Lighting a twisted stogie, he strolled back through the lobby and took the elevator up to his modest two-room suite.

Foxx wasted no time. Shaving quickly, he put on a fresh shirt and a brown fashionably cut suit and slipped his feet into a pair of lizard-skin walking boots made by McCurran in Denver. This morning he not only slid the Cloverleaf Colt into the pouch-holster that was tailored into all his coats, but belted on his American Model .38 Smith & Wesson as well.

Gray dawn light was just beginning to give way to a bright, sunny day when Foxx left the hotel. Refreshed by Archille's breakfast eggs, rid of the torn and dirty clothing he'd been wearing, Foxx started down Sansome toward Clay, heading for the brick building at Clay and Montgomery where the California & Kansas Railroad's main offices were located. He carried the sniper's rifle with him; until now, distractions had kept him from giving the weapon the close examination he'd planned.

When Foxx opened the massive front door of the C&K Building with his key, the only lights showing were from the telegraph room at the rear of the main floor. Foxx made his way down the wide hallway toward the telegraph room.

A tired-eyed operator, weary from his all-night vigil and impatient for his relief to show up, nodded to Foxx with a noticeable lack of enthusiasm. All the telegraphers knew that when the C&K's chief of detectives came to their office in person it usually preceded a period of frenzied activity.

"How many messages this morning, Mr. Foxx?" the telegrapher asked.

"Only one," Foxx replied, reaching for a green C&K company flimsy. "And it's just a duty notice to send a callboy from the roundhouse."

He scribbled the note rapidly. "Send callboy immediately 327 Simmons Street. Nat Green, detective divi-

sion, to report by cab to headquarters at once."
Scrawling his name at the bottom of the flimsy, Foxx
passed it to the telegrapher and started along the dimly
lit hall to the stairway leading to the second floor,
where his own office was located. The clacking of the
telegraph key began before he reached the stairs, and
he knew that he could look for Green to show up
within the hour.

In his office, Foxx pulled the chain that lit the acety-
lene lamp in the center of the ceiling. The lamp sputtered for a moment, then the mantle glowed and settled
down to a greenish-white cone of brilliant light. Putting
the rifle on the table that stood in front of his desk,
Foxx began his examination of the weapon.

Though the rifle showed signs of wear, it had been a
quality weapon before Foxx's bullet shattered the
stock. Foxx had identified it as soon as he'd picked it
up from the beach. The rifle was a Henry repeater with
its distinctive tubular magazine below the blued octago-
nal barrel. Now he levered out the magazine and discovered that the gun was chambered to take the heavy
.44 Sharps cartridge.

Foxx tested the trigger pull and found it steady and
even, the hammer dropping with an authoritative click
that indicated the action was in good shape. Turning
the rifle end-on-end, Foxx scrutinized the opened action more closely. He had advanced the loading lever,
which had brought the cocking rod out of its housing
at the top and rear of the action; the rod was now
pressed against a nock in the hammer, pushing the
hammer to full cock. The marks of fresh filing on the
rod caught Foxx's searching eyes. He ran a finger
along the rod, and felt an almost invisible ridge on its
surface, where it had been broken and repaired. Closer
inspection gave Foxx no other information. He filed the

fact away in his mind for future investigation and went on with his examination of the weapon.

The lever and other components of the action seemed to be in good condition, though the brass casing that enclosed the action bore a maze of scratches that told of long and frequent use. The gun was well oiled, and its blued metal barrel showed no signs of rust. The bluing was worn in a pattern that told Foxx it had been used as a saddle gun, which meant that its owner was not a city dweller.

Aside from these scanty facts Foxx could make no further deductions from the sniper's rifle. He closed the action, stood the gun in a corner of his office, and settled back to wait for Nat Green.

Green arrived in less than the hour Foxx had estimated. The C&K detective listened attentively while Foxx explained his assignment, then asked, "Suppose I tackle some innocent citizen who gets too close to Mrs. Martin? Is the C&K going to square things for me?"

"Don't worry, the C&K will square up any trouble you might get into, Nat. The only thing you've got to worry about is keeping that lady from getting hurt, and I don't give a damn how many times you step on innocent citizens' toes while you're doing it. And if you see some really suspicious character, don't waste any time putting the cuffs on him."

Green nodded. "All right. I'll do my best to keep her safe."

"I'm sure you will. Now get on over to Larkin Street and stay on the job until your relief shows up this evening."

After Green had gone, Foxx leaned back in his chair and lit a fresh stogie. He closed his eyes while he planned a course of action. He was just starting to work out a scheme when sleeplessness and exhaustion caught up with him.

Foxx woke with a start. Wondering how long he'd been sleeping, he took out his Pailliard Repeater and checked the time. The hands pointed to eight, and when he stepped into the hall he saw that the chief of the C&K's railroad police was just entering his office.

"Jim!" Foxx called. "We've got to have a talk, right this minute!"

Flaherty looked around. "I thought you'd be on your way up to Idaho Territory by now," he said, frowning. "Weren't you supposed to leave at six?"

"I was, but something's happened that kept me here."

"It'd better be important," Flaherty warned as Foxx followed him into the office and closed the door. "That mess over in Idaho's not going to wait forever."

"It's important," Foxx replied.

Leaving out the details of his activities with Vida Martin, Foxx gave Flaherty a summary of the sniper's attack at the Cliff House and what had happened afterward. When he'd finished, the chief of the railroad police sat silently for a long minute, his lips compressed.

"Does Caleb know you've been going out with his wife's sister?" he asked Foxx.

"Vida's a grown woman, Jim, even if she is Clara Petersen's younger sister. But we never tried to keep it secret that we go out together once in a while when I'm in town. I'd guess that Caleb and Clara know what's going on."

"Well, then, I don't see that there's a lot to get stirred up about," Flaherty said thoughtfully. "All you've got to do is have one of your men keep an eye on Mrs. Martin until we catch up with whoever's after you."

"I've already got Nat Green standing guard at Vida's flat," Foxx said. "I don't think you get the idea though, Jim. Clara Petersen's next of kin to Vida. Whoever that sniper is, he's after the people he thinks I got some attachments to. That'd include Clara and maybe Caleb, too. Hell, for all I know, you might even be on his list yourself."

"Now, wait a minute!" Flaherty began. He stopped short, his face puckered into a thoughtful frown. "I see how you got it figured, Foxx. That sniper's the kind of lunatic that wrecks trains because he's got a grudge against the railroad. He won't care how many people he kills to get revenge on you."

"That's about it."

"The question is, where do we start looking for this maniac?"

"I've got some ideas about that," Foxx replied. "And if you'll go along with them, I think they'll get me to that job in Idaho pretty fast."

"All right," Flaherty said. "Let's hear it."

For the next ten minutes Foxx talked quickly as he explained his plan to Flaherty. When he'd finished, the chief of the railroad police leaned back in his chair and thought for a moment. Then he said, "It's risky as hell, Foxx. If your scheme doesn't work, I don't need to tell you what's going to bust loose."

"No, you don't have to tell me, Jim," Foxx smiled grimly. "I know what I'm letting myself in for if it don't work. But as chancy as it is, it's the only thing I could come up with. We've got to move fast."

"All right, Foxx, go ahead with your scheme. I'll get my clerk making up the list you'll need." Flaherty paused and shook his head. "I'm not so sure I like the idea. But if it works, it'll keep Caleb and Clara out of danger, and your friend Mrs. Martin, too. I wish you luck. You'll need it."

During the next two hours Foxx drove the operators in the C&K's telegraph room to the point of nervous breakdown. Because Western Union had not yet been successful in extending its operations more than a few score miles west of the Mississippi, the only facilities that could provide fast nationwide communications were the railroad telegraph lines. These lines were not formally interconnected, but in an emergency the railroads forgot their rivalries and helped one another out by setting up temporary connections at key points across the country where two railroads maintained offices.

Within several hours Foxx had prodded the chief telegrapher to persuade the Union Pacific, the Santa Fe, and the Chicago Northwestern to interconnect their lines in order to give Foxx a direct wire from the C&K's San Francisco office into the main office of the Pinkerton National Detective Agency in Chicago.

Ten minutes after the connection with Pinkerton's had been established, Foxx was swapping messages with his old friend Romy Dehon. It took him only a few minutes to explain his needs, and an even shorter time for Romy to assure him that Pinkerton's could and would take care of them.

Before another hour had passed, using the list Flaherty's clerk had compiled, Foxx had a second list, much shorter, of eleven convicts imprisoned for crimes against the C&K who had been released from four Western penitentiaries within the past six months. Carrying his list, Foxx went back to his office and lit a stogie.

An hour later he'd narrowed the suspects down to

four. Picking up the sniper's rifle, Foxx left the office, determined to narrow the list to one name.

At the gunsmithing shop of Liddell & Kedding, Foxx showed the rifle to Kedding. "I was wondering if you might've done the job of fixing up the cocking rod," he said, pushing the lever down to bring the rod out against the hammer. He pointed to the almost invisible hairline and ridge that marked the repair.

Kedding took the rifle from Foxx and scrutinized the rod. He shook his head. "Not my work, Foxx," he said. "I'd know it, if it was. But this is the first one of these old Henrys that I've seen for ten years. Whoever fixed it'd be sure to remember, if he did the work lately."

"You got any suggestions?"

"Try Olaf Gunderson, over on Post Street," Kedding replied. "It's good work. Outside of us and Gunderson and Ed Barton, there's not another shop in town that can do such a neat job."

Gunderson recognized the rifle the instant Foxx showed it to him. "Ya, of course," he said, peering through the spectacles that perched dangerously close to the tip of his broad beet-red nose. "A veek ago, maybe only fife days, I make this work."

"What'd the fellow look like who brought the gun in?"

Gunderson scratched his head. "Not a young man he vass, but not old, too. Forty, maybe. Smallpox scars he has on his face. A big mouth, ugly. A big man, too, Foxx, bigger from you or me either vun. Vhy? You think he's maybe crook? He rob the railroad from something?"

Foxx did not answer at once. Gunderson's description of the rifle's owner—the sniper—had jogged his memory. He thought back several years to a time when a ragtag gang of outlaws had derailed a C&K passenger train at a bridge across the Republican River near the Colorado-Nebraska border. Foxx had been in charge of the C&K's detective force for only a few months then, and had continued his dogged pursuit of the outlaws long after the posse from Nebraska had given up the search.

Blake Morgan, the leader of the gang, had been crippled for life when his spine was shattered by a slug from Foxx's rifle during the gang's last-ditch fight. Jed Morgan, Blake's hulking son by his common-law wife, a Kiowa woman, had been captured and sent to prison. And Jedediah Morgan was one of the names on the list of released convicts that was in Foxx's pocket. Now Foxx had discovered the identity of his mortal foe.

"Thanks, Olaf," Foxx said, taking the rifle from the stocky gunsmith's hands. "You've been a big help— more help than you know." He started for the door, then had a thought and turned back to say, "Olaf. If the fellow you fixed this gun for should come in here to buy another one, I'd appreciate it if you'll let me know the minute he steps in your front door. Stall selling him a gun, if you can. I'll be here in a few minutes if I get the word he's showed up."

"You want him pretty bad, ya?" Gunderson asked.

"I want him the worst kind of way, Olaf. If he comes in and you don't have any way to send word to me, call a policeman and tell him I want that man arrested."

Gunderson nodded. "I vill remember, Foxx. If he comes in, I vill send my boy to tell you."

Back at his office, Foxx stayed at his desk only long enough to think his scheme through yet another time. Then he went to Flaherty's office, lighting a twisted stogie as he walked down the hall.

Flaherty didn't look up from the sheaf of papers in his hand. He growled, "Just a minute, Foxx. And do something about that damned cigar, will you? Chew it or put it out. If I thought you'd change to a better kind if you were making a bigger salary, I'd tell Jared Blossom to give you a raise."

"Well, I'd be glad for the money, Jim, but I don't think I'd change cigars." Foxx dropped the stogie in the spittoon that stood at the corner of Flaherty's desk.

"You look a little more cheerful than you did when you left," Flaherty said, putting the papers aside. "You must've had some luck."

"Call it what you want. I've found out the name of the man we're after."

"Who is he?"

"Jedediah Morgan. Blake Morgan's boy."

"I remember," Flaherty nodded. "That robbery at the river in Nebraska a few years ago. He's out of the pen, then?"

"Out and after my hide. He's part Kiowa. That's why he's going about this thing the way he is." Seeing Flaherty's puzzled expression, Foxx explained, "Kiowas who're out to get back at an enemy will go after his relatives or a member of his clan if they can't get to him."

"Now, that doesn't make any sense, Foxx!"

"It might not to one of us. To a Kiowa it does. He also probably figured that Vida'd get word to me, which would give him the pleasure of watching me sweat."

"Well, I'll take your word for that. What did Pinkerton's come up with?"

"They're sending out a woman operative. I described Vida to Romy Dehon as best I could, and she says she's got a woman who looks enough like Vida to pass, if we put a red wig on her."

"No trouble about that," Flaherty smiled. "As far as I can tell, half the women in this town wear a wig or a false hairpiece of some kind."

"That's what I'm counting on. The Pinkerton's woman is on the way to San Francisco right now. She ought to be here day after tomorrow."

"How're you going to switch the Pinkerton op for Mrs. Martin without Jed Morgan catching on?"

"Did you ever read a story called *The Purloined Letter*? It's by a man named Poe."

Flaherty shook his head. "I'm not much for reading."

"Neither am I," Foxx admitted. "I ran across this one in a book somebody left on the Flyer. But what the story's really about is how to hide something." Seeing Flaherty's bewilderment, Foxx went on. "In the story, there's a letter hidden just by putting it with a lot of other letters in a desk. In other words, if you've got something to hide, put it where it's so easy to see that nobody's going to pay any attention to it."

"What's that got to do with switching places with Mrs. Martin and the Pinkerton woman?" Flaherty frowned.

"With your help it'll work like this: You'll take the Pinkerton op into Vida's flat, and she'll be a blonde, her real hair color. But inside, Vida's put on her blond wig. When you come out, Vida will be with you, but Morgan's going to think she's the same blonde woman you went in the building with. You'll take Vida out and get her safe to Caleb's house, where she's going to stay—"

"Does Caleb know anything about this?" Flaherty broke in.

"Not yet. I'm counting on Vida and Clara breaking the news to him, and after it's explained, it'll all work out."

Flaherty shook his head. "I hope you're right about that."

"I am," Foxx said. He went on, "Now, when Vida's safe, you're going to wait an hour or so, go back to the flat, and this time you'll come out with the Pinkerton, who's got on a red wig and will look like Vida."

"Foxx, this is the silliest damned thing I ever heard!" Flaherty exploded. "Do you really think it'll fool Morgan?"

"I'm positive." Foxx's calm assurance was registered in his voice. "Morgan's going to be waiting for a red-haired woman to come out, and that's what he'll see. He won't be too close to you, remember. He'll follow you, thinking Vida will lead him to me."

Flaherty thought for a moment, then said reluctantly, "Well, it might just work, at that. It'd be about the same as a fish taking bait, I guess."

"That's the whole idea!" Foxx agreed. "Now, the Pinkerton woman and you will head for the depot. We'll give Morgan all the time he needs to follow you. He'll see us meet at the ferry slip, while we're waiting for the Oakland boat to pull out, and if he misses us there, he can hire a boat to take him across the bay and get on the Flyer at Oakland. All the time Nat Green will be following him. You can just bet Morgan's going to get on that train with us."

"Yep. I suppose he will," Flaherty admitted.

"Between here and Sacramento, I'll arrest Morgan. It'll happen on railroad property, so nobody's going to question my right. Nat will bring him back here to stand trial for trying to kill me and Vida at the Cliff House, and I'll go on to Idaho on my case."

Gazing at Foxx with something between perplexity and surprise, Flaherty shook his head slowly. "You make it sound awfully easy, Foxx. I just hope it works out the way you've planned it."

CHAPTER 4

"Do you think we fooled your man, Foxx?" Maxine Bowden asked.

Foxx and the female Pinkerton operative were sitting at a table in the parlor car in the C&K's eastbound Flyer. The train had just pulled away from the ferry slip at Carquinez Strait and was now skirting the little town of Benicia as it began its run across the semi-marshland that lay between San Pablo Bay and the state capital at Sacramento.

"I ain't seen him, if that's what you mean. It's been a spell of years since I looked at Jed Morgan, and he might've changed more'n I figured. You know how it is in this business, Maxine. There's times when you'll recognize somebody from their description, but not know them right off when you come face to face with them." ·

Looking at Maxine Bowden, Foxx was struck again by the remarkable resemblance between the Pinkerton's woman operative and Vida Martin. Skillful makeup and the red wig she was wearing heightened the resemblance. As far as Foxx knew, Morgan had never seen Vida at close quarters, and he was certain the switch had deceived the outlaw.

"How can you be sure this man Morgan got on the train, if you didn't see him, Foxx?" she asked.

"When you put it that way, I can't be. But I'll lay you a bet Morgan's on this train."

"How can you be so sure, if you didn't see him at the Oakland depot?"

"You won't see a man like Morgan when he don't want you to," Foxx replied. "He got that from his mother's side of the family, I'd imagine."

"His mother was a criminal too?"

"No. She was a Kiowa Indian, and Kiowas are almost as good as Comanches and Apaches when it comes to skulking around without being noticed."

"I wouldn't know. I'm a city girl; this is my first time west of Omaha."

"How'd you get hooked up with Pinkerton's?" Foxx asked.

Maxine shrugged. "I suppose you'd say I inherited my husband's job. He'd been with Allan Pinkerton a long time before he got killed in a gunfight with a gang of safecrackers. That was two years ago. Allan had seen that Romy Dehon was doing a good job as an operative, so he hired me."

"When I saw Romy the last time, on a case that we was both working in a little town over in Kansas, she said Pinkerton was thinking about putting more women on his force. You like the work?"

"It's better than most jobs a woman can hope to get. I don't like to cook or clean house, and I don't sew. I've got to do some kind of work, and this does beat housework or clerking in a general store."

"That doesn't sound to me like you enjoy your job much," Foxx commented.

"Some cases I like to work on, some I don't. This one, now, looks like it'll be interesting. I've heard so much about San Francisco that I've always wanted to see it, and your lady friend gave me these clothes, which are a lot nicer than anything I can afford on the salary I get."

"You did a good job. I'll see the word gets passed up to your boss."

"Thanks, Foxx. But don't make any promises you can't keep. Let's wait and see how this case turns out. I'd feel a lot better if we were sure that Morgan's really on the train."

"I'm certain he is, and you'll find out I'm right in just about two minutes. Here comes Nat Green, and if I know Nat, he hasn't let Morgan out of his sight for a minute."

Green passed through the parlor car without seeming to notice Foxx and Maxine Bowden, but as he went by the table where they sat he gestured to Foxx, a quick lifting of his finger, pointing to the observation platform at the back of the car. Foxx gave no indication that he'd noticed the slight flicking of Green's forefinger. After waiting several moments, he took a stogie out of his pocket, and leaned across the table.

"I'll go talk to Nat," he said in a low voice. "He didn't want to sit down with us, so I guess he's on to something."

Foxx stood up. Lighting his stogie and moving unhurriedly, he strolled to the back of the car and went out to the observation platform. Nat Green was waiting, watching the door.

"Have you seen Jed Morgan?" he asked Foxx.

"No. I haven't been up toward the front of the train at all. Which car's he sitting in?"

"None of them."

"You mean you lost him?"

"It looks like I have for right now," Green confessed.

"He's not on the train?"

"Oh, he's on the train, I'm positive of that. He's just found himself a place to hole up. I imagine he's afraid you'll recognize him if you get a look at him."

Foxx controlled the sudden surge of anger that swept over him. His voice level, he asked Green, "When was the last time you saw him?"

"Just as the train pulled out after we'd crossed on the Carquinez ferry. He was in the second car with me. I looked out the window for a minute, and when I looked back into the car, he'd—well, he'd just disappeared."

"You've been through all the cars, I guess?"

"Sure. I went forward as far as the baggage car, then back to the smoker. It's right in front of this car."

"And Morgan wasn't anyplace you looked?"

Green shook his head despondently. "Damn it, Foxx, there's no way that son of a bitch could've hidden from me! I went through every damned coach, and he wasn't in any of them!"

Foxx puffed at his stogie in silence for a moment, then said, "Let's go back to the beginning, Nat, and take it step by step up to where you lost him."

"All right. When Flaherty and the Pinkerton woman came out of Vida Martin's flat, Morgan was across the street and about two houses down from the building her flat's in. I was across the street from him."

"You're sure he didn't spot you then?"

"I'm sure, Foxx. Morgan had a hack waiting, but he wasn't in it, so I could see him plain enough. I was in a closed hack, so I'm damn sure he didn't see me. His hack was headed toward the bay, mine wasn't. When Flaherty and the Pinkerton op—"

"Her name's Maxine Bowden, Nat," Foxx said.

Green nodded. "When those two came out, Morgan got in the hack. Their driver turned right around and started toward the bay and Morgan waited until they passed him to tell his hackie to follow theirs. I had my driver turn as quick as he could and got right behind Morgan's hack. I let him get started for the bay ferry and kept behind him. I followed him on the boat, and since I knew he couldn't get off until we'd crossed the bay, I made myself scarce so he wouldn't catch on that I was on his tail."

"You picked him up in Oakland, then?" Foxx asked when Green paused for breath.

"Sure. I got off the ferry first and stood where I could watch the gangplank. I saw you and the—you and Miss Bowden meet, and Morgan was in the crowd a little way back of you. He started for the Flyer, and I tagged along behind him. I got a seat in the same car."

"You don't think he tumbled to you following him?"

"If he did, he didn't act like it. Like I said a minute ago, I had him in sight until about two minutes before the Flyer pulled out after we'd crossed. He didn't move out of his seat while the crew broke the train to get it on the Carquinez Strait ferry, and he didn't stir while we crossed. Then—well, in that minute I looked out the window, he just disappeared, Foxx. It didn't bother me at first, but when he didn't come back when the train started, I got bothered and began looking for him."

Foxx shook his head. "We've got to be missing something, Nat. There's no way he could've got off that train. Standing orders is to keep the coach and vestibule doors locked from the time a passenger train stops for Carquinez until it pulls out on the other side of the strait."

More to himself than to Foxx, Nat Green said, "He could've gone out a window, I guess, but if he'd done that, the passengers or one of the crew would've seen him."

"Yes," Foxx agreed. "The coaches oughta be pretty well filled, from what I noticed at Oakland."

"They are. I ought to know. I checked all of them, even the toilets, men's and women's both. There was a woman in one of them, and I guess I shocked her out of a year's growth, but—"

"Wait a minute, Nat!" Foxx exclaimed. "That's what we've been missing! The Carquinez crossing's not a station stop. They don't lock up the toilets like they do at a station. Did you notice a window open in any of the toilets?"

Frowning, Green scratched his head. "Damned if I can remember now. I wasn't looking for open windows, but you're right. Morgan could've gotten out of a toilet window without any of the passengers seeing him."

Foxx went on. "The train crew, they'd be busy recoupling, and the conductor and brakie would be off the train too. The porter would be someplace in the cars, but he'd be tending to his own business, he wouldn't be expecting somebody to skin out of a toilet window."

"So if that's how Morgan got away from me, where's he hiding now?" Green asked.

"I can think of three places without half trying," Foxx replied without hesitating. "The rods, or up top, or the blind baggage."

The tie rods ran under the coaches and tied the body of the coach to the running gear; the cartops, on which a man could lie down and keep himself in place by clinging to the slatted wooden walkway, ran the length of each coach; and the closed-off vestibule at the front end of the baggage car, just behind the tender, was called the "blind baggage" because it could not be seen readily from either the coaches or the engine cab. All three spots were favored by hobos who chose to get their free transportation on the speedy passenger trains instead of riding in an empty boxcar on a slower freight train.

"If he's up top or in the blinds, we can find him right fast," Green said thoughtfully. "There's no way to check on the rods until we stop in Sacramento."

"There's nothing to stop us looking up top or in the blinds right now," Foxx told the detective. "Come on, Nat. Let's see if we can locate the slick bastard."

First Foxx, then Green, swung off the side of the vestibule onto the rungs of the climb-bars that led to the top of the coach. Once they were on the walkway, the entire length of the train was visible, but Morgan was not on any of the cars.

Swaying in rhythm with the shifting of the coaches, pulling their hats down to keep the wind from snatching them away, the two men walked the length of the train, jumping the four-foot gap between the cars with the ease of long familiarity. At the head of the train they made the final leap from the front of the baggage car, but Morgan was not in the blind spot in the front vestibule of the baggage car either.

"That leaves the rods," Foxx said as they hunched their backs to the swift chilly wind sweeping across the stubby tender. "It'd have been easy enough for Morgan to've dropped out one of the toilet windows and ducked under the coach. The crew would've been too busy to notice him."

"There's no way to check the rods now that we're movin'," Green said. "So we can't be sure Morgan's there until we get to Sacramento."

"It's the only place he could be," Foxx pointed out. "And I don't think we need to worry about him getting off before we stop. We might as well go back inside, Nat. There ain't a thing we can do standing here, and that wind's getting pretty cold."

Making the high swing back up to the top of the baggage coach, they walked the length of the car and descended to the vestibule of the first coach. Inside, they went into the men's toilet at the front of the coach to wash off the gritty bits of coal ash that they'd picked up on their hands and faces during their search.

While Foxx waited for Green to finish drying his hands, he lit a stogie and said thoughtfully through the cloud of blue smoke, "There'll be five of us watching when we slow down in Sacramento, and I don't think all of us could miss seeing Jed Morgan when he rolls out from under whatever car he's on."

"Five?" Green frowned.

"You, me, and Maxine makes three. The conductor and the brakie both carry pistols, they'll be the other two."

Green's jaw dropped in surprise. "You'd put a woman on a job like that?"

"A Pinkerton woman, Nat. She's supposed to hold up her end of a job just like a man would."

"Well, you're the boss. If you say so, I guess it's all right. But if I ever go out on a case with a female detective, I'd want to have my head examined."

"I don't say I'd hire a woman for the C&K," Foxx said. "But Pinkerton's is in a little bit different situation, Nat. They handle a lot of cases where a woman might come in real handy."

"That might be," Green said as he and Foxx started back to the parlor car. "But when you come right down to it, Foxx, there's some jobs a woman can't handle."

"I'd give a lot to know where you've been, Foxx,"

Maxine Bowden greeted them when they reached the parlor car. "I went through this train twice from one end to the other, and you'd both disappeared the way Jed Morgan did."

"We had to go up on top of the train," Foxx explained. "I didn't expect to be gone long enough to worry you."

"I wasn't exactly worried," she said. "But I thought you'd better take a look at this."

Lifting her purse from the table, she took out a folded sheet of coarse blue-lined paper and handed it to Foxx. Even before he'd unfolded it, Foxx recognized the paper as the same kind on which Morgan's note to Vida had been written. When he looked at the note, he recognized the handwriting as well.

"It aint no use you trieing to run away, Vida Martin," the note read. "Foxx being along woent stop me from killing you. You woent no when, but Ill get you whin Ime ready to. Foxx doent get his till later on."

"Where the devil did you get this, Maxine?" Foxx demanded, handing the note to Green to read.

"Right after you left, the porter handed it to me. As soon as I'd read it, I started looking for you."

"Did you think to ask the porter where he got it?" Green asked.

"Of course I did," Maxine answered. "That was the first thing I did. He said a man gave him a half-dollar to deliver it to me, just before the train went across the river on that big ferryboat."

Foxx asked her quickly, "You didn't ask him to point out the man?"

"No. I thought that if I did, Morgan might decide to kill me now, and if he got any ideas like that, I wanted you men to be there to stop him."

"You're not carrying a gun, then?" Green asked.

"I certainly am!" she replied. "But I've got sense enough to know that an experienced criminal like this man Morgan can probably outshoot me. I haven't had too much practice with a pistol."

"You showed pretty good sense, I'd say," Green told her.

To stop what he thought might become a dispute between Green and Maxine, Foxx said, "Nat, go find that porter and bring him back here. I wanta hear what he's got to say."

When Green returned with the porter, Foxx showed his badge to the man and said, "You gave a note to this young lady, a note a man back at Carquinez Strait asked you to deliver."

"Yessir, Mr. Foxx. He did, and I did, just like you say."

"What'd the man look like?"

"Oh, he was a big one! And ugly! Lawd, I don't know when I seen an uglier white man! Had a sorta dark skin and his face was all scarred up, the smallpox, I guess. And a mean mouth. But he give me a half-dollar, so I done what he said."

"Have you seen that man since then?"

For a moment the porter's shining black face twisted in thought, then he shook his head. "Well, now, that's a right funny thing, come to think about hit. I ain't seen him since then."

"You didn't see him get off?" Green asked.

"No, sir. And that's funny, too, because we ain't made no stops since the strait."

Foxx had been prepared for the porter's reply. He said, "All right, Jimmy. Thanks for helping us out. And if you see that man again before we get to Sacramento, don't act like you're surprised, just get back here as fast as you can and tell me."

"Yessir, Mr. Foxx! I'll do exac'ly like you says!"

When the porter had gone, Foxx told his companions, "Well, we're pretty sure that Morgan's still on the Flyer. Now all we've got to do is stop him from killing somebody before we can get hold of him."

"How do we do that?" Green asked. "We think he's riding the rods under one of the coaches, but we don't know which one it is. There're fifteen coaches on this drag, and even with what help we can get from the crew, we can't cover all fifteen at the same time."

Foxx consulted his Pailliard Repeater and said, "We won't be pulling into Sacramento for an hour and a half. That oughta give us plenty of time to come up with something that'll work."

Foxx, Nat Green, and Maxine Bowden spent the next ninety minutes devising a plan to capture Jed Morgan. Five minutes before the Flyer reached the Sacramento yards, when they put the finishing touches to their scheme, it seemed simple and foolproof.

Foxx rarely used the blanket authority his position gave him on C&K trains and crews, but this time he invoked it to carry out the plan. As the Flyer reached the "Yard Limit" sign that stood beside the main-line tracks, the engineer eased the throttle down until the train was creeping along, but still moving fast enough to make it impossible for a man riding the rods to leave the train without the wheels of the coaches catching him before he could get clear.

When they neared the first switch that would shunt the train off to an isolated sidetrack, the fireman leaped from the cab and ran ahead to throw the switch. The Flyer swerved away from the depot and headed for the edge of the yards without slowing further. When it had reached a spot far from the center of the yards, the engineer brought the train to an abrupt halt.

To place both sides of the Flyer under observation, Foxx had stationed the conductor and baggagemaster in the vestibule of the first coach, each positioned to drop to the ground on a different side of the train. Nat Green and the brakeman were on the observation car, also on opposite sides of the coach. For himself Foxx had chosen a car near the center, and depended on luck to choose the correct side on which to step off.

Maxine, still wearing Vida's clothing and the red wig, had been standing on the vestibule step, waiting for the train to stop. She dropped to the ground and started away from the train at a fast walk. The moment she left the train, the men dropped to the ground with their pistols ready in their hands, their eyes searching the open space between the coaches and the rails, where Morgan would have to emerge when he came off the rods to get a clear shot at Maxine.

Seconds ticked away as they stood with their weapons poised, ready to shoot, but Morgan did not appear in the space below the coaches. Foxx hunkered down and called to the brakeman on the other side of the train, "Any sign of him over there?"

"Not hair nor hide," the trainman replied. "But I'm ready if he shows up!"

Foxx stood up, slowly lowering his gun hand. "We might as well call it off," he told the others. "If Morgan was under there, he'd've moved before now." Raising his voice, he called, "Maxine! Come on back! We've been skunked!"

Slowly, Maxine turned and started back toward the train. When she came within voice range, she said tartly, "Foxx, the next time you go looking for a target, don't look at me! I've never felt so damned exposed in my life before! It wouldn't have been so bad, if it hadn't all been wasted. What happened to Morgan?"

"I'd give just about anything you can name to know, myself. He just wasn't where we figured he'd be, that's all."

"Where is he, then?" Green demanded, his voice edgy.

"That's what we're going to have to find out," Foxx said. He broke off as the baggagemaster came through the vestibule, his pistol dangling from his hand. A few moments later the brakeman rounded the end of the last car and stood beside Green, both of them looking along the train to where Foxx was standing.

"I heard you telling your people we had a water haul, Mr. Foxx," the brakeman said. "How come the fellow we were looking for didn't show up?"

"That's what we're all wondering," Foxx snapped. "I'll talk to you and the rest of the train crew when we get to the depot. Now, suppose you go tell the conductor it's all right to pull up where he's supposed to be right now."

Foxx turned to Maxine, who was standing disconsolately beside the coach. "It ain't the end of the world," he told her, forcing a calm note into his voice. "Jed Morgan just outsmarted us this time, that's all."

CHAPTER 5

Foxx looked across the table at Maxine and Green. They'd gone back into the parlor car after the aborted effort to take Jed Morgan, and now the Flyer was creeping backward at a snail's pace as it returned to the main line.

"Let's don't waste time trying to figure out what went wrong, or where Morgan found a place to hide, or anything else," Foxx said. "My guess is he's still on the Flyer, in some hidey-hole we haven't thought of."

"I wish I was as sure about that as you sound," Green grumbled. "Seems to me like we covered all the hiding places there are on this train."

"Don't forget Morgan's half Kiowa, Nat. Like I told Maxine a little while ago, a Kiowa or Apache or Comanche can hide behind a grain of sand, and a white man will look right at him and swear there's not an Indian within ten miles."

"I believe you now, Foxx," Maxine put in. "But if he's so good, he could have gotten off the train without our seeing him."

"I could be wrong," Foxx admitted. "It wouldn't be the first time, if I am. But I'm going by what that porter said. If you recall, he told us that Morgan gave him that note addressed to Vida while the train was on the ferry at Carquinez. Well, the Flyer just hasn't slowed down enough since then for Morgan to jump off."

"With all of us looking for him here, I'll grant you he couldn't've gotten off where we stopped on the siding," Green said thoughtfully. "Maybe you're right at that, Foxx. He might've just stayed wherever he's holed up."

"I'm just as glad he didn't come out, I think," Maxine said. Her voice was much calmer than it had been when she talked to Foxx the last time. "I've never been shot at, and I don't know how I'd've acted if he'd started shooting at me."

"Him staying hid sorta puts me in between a rock and a hard place," Foxx told the others. "The only way Flaherty would agree to me trying this scheme was for me to go on up to Idaho after we caught Morgan. I was supposed to be up there two days ago, so I've got to keep on going."

"I won't be much help to you on a railroad case," Maxine said. "I guess that means I'll be going on back to Chicago."

Foxx shook his head. "Not yet. Jed Morgan's not after me right now; he's said so. He's after Vida Martin, and as long as he thinks you're Vida, he's going to follow you. You'll have to go right along to Idaho with me. I don't think you've got much choice."

"That makes good sense," Nat Green said. "And it'll be a lot easier for us to spot him in open country than it would in a crowded place like San Francisco."

"But that's what you're going to have to try to do, though, Nat. I'll send a wire while we're here and have Griff Presser come over to Winnemucca from Elko to be my backup man."

"Now, wait a minute, Foxx!" Green protested. "I thought I was on this case with you till it's closed!"

"You are. But that note of Morgan's might be just a trick to make us think Maxine fooled him, while he caught on somewhere along the way that Vida's still in San Francisco."

"Does that mean you think I fell down on my assignment?" Maxine bristled. "Look here, Foxx, I did my best! And you told me yourself that I'd've fooled you."

"You did every bit as good as I said you did, too," Foxx assured her. "But I underrated this man before, so maybe I also just talked myself into thinking our trick would work on Jed Morgan."

"Well," she shrugged, "the C&K's paying Pinkerton's as long as I'm on the case, so I guess it's up to you. It doesn't make any difference to me whether I work in Idaho or Chicago. At least I'll see a lot of the West."

"You're on the case until it's closed, Maxine. If you did fool Morgan, you'll have to stick with me and keep fooling him until we catch him."

"Then I ought to stay on the case too," Green insisted.

"No, Nat. We've got to cover all the angles."

"What other angles are there to worry about? Morgan's after Vida, and he thinks that's who Maxine is. As soon as we get into open country, where he can't hide so easily, we'll take him."

"Look at it the other way, Nat," Foxx said. "Suppose Maxine didn't fool Morgan? If he's found out he followed the wrong woman, he might be heading back to San Francisco right now. You're the only man in the division who knows what Jed Morgan looks like, and that's why I want you to go back and stand guard over Vida until we find out for sure where he is."

Green looked frustrated for a moment, then agreed.

"Well, that makes sense too. But, damn it, Foxx, when are we going to be sure of anything in this case?"

"When we've got Jed Morgan back behind bars again." Foxx took out a stogie and lit it before adding, "And the way he's been running circles around us, it looks like it might take a little while to do that."

"My God, I didn't realize how big this country is," Maxine told Foxx as they stood on the platform of the C&K's little station at Winnemucca the following day.

"There's a lot of open space to it, all right," Foxx agreed. "I been used to it as long as I remember, so it don't look as funny to me as it would to you, I guess."

Maxine looked at the fifty or sixty buildings that made up the little town. About a dozen of them were occupied by business establishments: stores, saloons, a restaurant, a livery stable. The other structures, most of them clustered around the business buildings on the south side of the C&K tracks, were residential dwellings. Outside the town barren ground stretched as far as they could see in every direction.

On the north side of the tracks railroad sidings ran ten tracks deep, sidings on which stood flatcars, freight cars, and gondolas. A single track ran north from the sidings, its shining rails dwindling to a straight thread of silver before they disappeared over the low line of ragged hills that broke the horizon.

"I hope that restaurant's food tastes better than the building looks," she said to Foxx. "I'm starving."

"Well, you won't get a meal like you would at the Parker House in Chicago, but you can get a platter of bacon and eggs or a decent bowl of stew here. Come on. We've got a while to wait; we might as well eat something. I could use a bite myself."

Foxx picked up Maxine's suitcase and his own. As

they walked along the baked earth of the rutted narrow road she said, "I don't know much about the railroad business, Foxx, but how can there be enough passengers traveling in and out of a place this size for the C&K to make any money by stopping here?"

"It's not passengers that we're looking for," Foxx explained to her. "It's the freight we haul over the spur line that runs north out of Winnemucca to the mines around Goldsburgh, up in Idaho Territory. Ore coming out, machinery going in, that's what makes this place pay off. Oh, there's a few passengers, miners and prospectors, but the freight's where the money is."

"Goldsburgh. That's where we're going?"

"That's where my case is."

They reached the restaurant and were served ham and eggs by the thin, tired-looking man who seemed to be cook, waiter, dishwasher, and general factotum. Their meal was neither good nor bad, but it did still the gnawing of their stomachs. Foxx led the way toward the row of sidings as they left the cafe.

Maxine looked at the lines of freight cars and said to Foxx, "Not that it makes any difference, but I've been wondering how we're going to get where we're headed for. I don't see any locomotives around."

"There'll be one in just before dark, hauling ore down from the mines. It'll haul machinery and stuff going back, and we'll be leaving on it too."

"Not in a boxcar, I hope."

"Not hardly. We'll ride in an accommodation car."

"What in the world is that?"

Foxx pointed to a coach that stood a little apart on a siding just ahead of them. "There it is right there. It's half passenger coach and half baggage car. It ain't exactly a parlor car, but it's comfortable enough."

"How far is Goldsburgh?"

"Oh, a hundred miles or so. Just a good day's haul for a freight train with a full load."

They reached the accommodation car, and Foxx helped Maxine up the first high step, then followed her into the car. A partition divided it from the baggage section; the half in which they stood was furnished with a wide divan, a table, and two or three easy chairs. Hooks for clothing were fastened high on one wall. Small, square curtained windows were set high in the walls on both sides of the coach, and a small pot-bellied stove stood in one corner.

"Make yourself at home," Foxx invited. "Griff Presser oughta get here from Elko in an hour or so. He'll go up with us. I've got to find out from him what this case is all about."

"If all we have to do is wait, I think I'll take a rest. That big divan looks really inviting." She looked at Foxx questioningly. "Is it all right if I take off this red wig until we get to where somebody can see us? That would be the most restful thing I can think of."

"I don't suppose it'd hurt. Wherever Jed Morgan is, he sure ain't in Winnemucca."

"No. He'd be easy to spot in a place this small." Maxine took off the wig and put it on the table. She unwound the silk scarf she'd been wearing, turban-like, under the wig and shook out her long blond hair. "Oh, that feels good. I think I'm just going to stretch out on this divan and nap for a while."

"You do that. I might catch forty winks myself, in one of them easy chairs, while we're waiting for Griff. But I sleep light. If anybody gets close, I'll rouse you."

Maxine was asleep almost as soon as she'd lain down on the divan. Foxx lowered himself into one of the deep-cushioned chairs and closed his eyes, but sleep evaded him. He lit a twisted stogie and opened his bag, took out the bottle of Cyrus Noble he'd had the foresight to pack, and drank a swallow from the bottle. Then he hung up his coat and hat, laid his Smith & Wesson on the floor beside his chair, and this time managed to doze off.

The sound of a locomotive giving the two sharp blasts that signaled a train's departure partially penetrated Foxx's sleep, but the tooting was too distant and too familiar a sound to awaken him completely. Foxx stirred in his chair, and was sinking back into full sleep again when the grating of bootsoles on the gravel roadbed outside the coach brought him fully awake.

Foxx's hand was scooping his revolver up from the floor beside the chair before his eyes were completely open. He was facing the door when the rapping of knuckles on its thick panels roused Maxine from her nap. She sat up, saw Foxx poised with the S&W in his hand, and reached for her purse, on the floor beside the divan.

"Foxx?" a man's voice called. "Can I come in?"

Foxx replied, "Sure, Griff. Come ahead." To Maxine he said, "It's my detective from Elko."

Presser came in, a tall man, his broad chest tapering to a narrow waist. His face was deeply tanned, his eyes light gray. He wore a dark brown Arizona-creased Stetson, and a tan cordcloth suit, with pointed range boots showing below the cuffless edges of the narrow trouser legs.

"I wasn't really sure you'd gotten here yet," Presser said as he and Foxx shook hands. "But I didn't want to bust in on you without knocking. I'm glad I didn't too; I'd have disturbed the young lady."

Foxx turned to Maxine. "Maxine, this is Griff Presser; you've heard me mention him. Griff, Miss

Bowden's a Pinkerton operative from Chicago. She's helping me on a case you haven't heard about yet."

"I've got a case you haven't heard about, too," Presser said. "A brand-new one."

"Sit down and have a drink before you tell me anything," Foxx said. He extended the bottle of Cyrus Noble to Presser, then in afterthought turned to Maxine and said, "Unless you'd like a sip first."

"I'd rather have my own," she replied. "Whiskey's not my favorite drink." She rummaged in her bag and took out a small silver flask. "That's why I carry a little gin with me."

Foxx lit a stogie and sat down. Presser handed him the bottle of bourbon and he downed a swallow. "Now," he told the Elko detective, "tell me about the wreckings first."

"What's happening is that the C&K's caught in the middle of a mining fight, Foxx," Presser began. "You know about the big syndicates in Butte and Boise—" Foxx nodded and Presser continued, "Well, they've fought to a draw. They're leaving each other alone right at the moment, resting up until they get ready to start a new battle, but while they're catching their breath, they're both trying to swallow up as many of the little independent mines as they can."

"I figured it might be something like that," Foxx nodded. "I've heard about the way the copper trust took over just about all the mines in Montana."

"A lot of the mines we're concerned with are owned by the Montana trust, Foxx," Presser said. "And the new syndicate in Boise is just as bad."

"I guess it's the same old story," Foxx said, frowning. "The big fellows are trying to bust the little ones by keeping 'em from getting the machinery they need for their crushers and loaders and all the rest of it.

And the easy way to stop 'em is to wreck the trains that's hauling in the stuff. Am I right?"

"From the way you talk, you've seen something like this happen before," Presser replied.

"Something real close to it, in the mining business up in the hill country of California, where the big placers are riding over the little one-man claims, wiping 'em out wherever they get in the way."

"I suppose it'd be the same situation," Presser said. "But it's not just the syndicates who're trying to keep the little miners from getting equipment, Foxx. The little fellows are fighting back. They do half the wrecking, trying to keep parts and new equipment from getting to the syndicate mines."

"Just how bad is it?" Foxx asked.

"It's serious," Presser said grimly. "There've been seven wrecks in the past ten weeks, four on the Bruneau River spur that runs from Winnemucca up to Goldsburgh, and three on the Sawtooth spur that runs from Elko to Picabo."

"Are you sure that some of those wrecks weren't legitimate accidents?"

"I'm sure. The super didn't get suspicious until the third wreck, so it took me a little while to check back on the first two. While I was checking, there were two more, and then before the super could report that the wrecks weren't accidents, two new ones. By then he'd sent a message to the construction super at the main office."

"How did he know none of the wrecks was caused by carelessness?"

"Tie plates taken off caused four wreckings and loosened fishplates the others. Now, there's no way in the world that our gandy dancers could've been that careless, Foxx."

"No," Foxx agreed. "Not at seven different places in such a short time. Those trains were all carrying machinery or spare parts to some of the mines?"

"Not all seven. Three of them were southbound ore-trains."

"How about the freight on the other four? Was it machinery for syndicate mines, or independent ones?"

"I guess you'd say it was even Stephen. Two shipments were to syndicate mines, the other two weren't. One of them wrecked a locomotive, and we had some cars busted up in all of them."

"Nobody been hurt or killed, though?"

"Not yet. But it's going to come down to that, if it goes on much longer. And from what I hear, it'll be likely to get worse, unless you can stop it."

"What've you heard?"

"A lot of stories. I don't know how true they are, but I'm ready to believe them. The syndicates—or maybe one of the syndicates, I can't prove anything—are supposed to be getting a bunch of hardcases together. Gunmen, outlaws, plug-uglies, you know the kind of men I'm talking about."

"A syndicate army, is that it?"

"Something like that. The men are supposed to be assembling right now at a hideout up in the Sawtooth Range. And the small miners are getting themselves an army too, from what I hear."

Maxine had been listening silently to the conversation between Foxx and Presser. Now she spoke for the first time. "Isn't there law of any kind out in this country?"

"Not a lot, Miss Bowden," Presser said. "Local sheriffs, local marshals."

"But what you're talking about sounds like a war! Can't you call in the Army?"

"By the time we got the pencil pushers in Washington moving, the war'd be over, Maxine."

"Well, if the local law can't do anything, and the Army won't do anything, what can you do about it, Foxx?"

"I don't know, yet. But if I don't do something, the C&K's going to lose a lot of money, so I got to try."

"I think I prefer living in a place where there's a police force," she said. "The one in Chicago might not be very good, but at least it's there when things go from bad to worse."

"I guess I know enough of the story now to sort things out," Foxx told Presser. "Let me do a little bit of thinking, and we can talk about it some more." He lit a fresh stogie and took another swallow of bourbon. "Now, what's this new case you started to tell me about a minute ago?"

"It's the damnedest thing I've ever seen, Foxx. Who'd want to steal a dead man's body?"

"From what I've heard, that was a pretty good business at one time," Foxx replied. "Stealing corpses for medical students to cut up and study."

"You know there's not a medical school between San Francisco and Kansas City, Foxx!" Presser said. "Besides, the bodies you're talking about were dug up in graveyards. This one was stolen from a C&K baggage car."

"You mean that happened at Elko, Griff?"

"No. The body wasn't stolen there, and I don't know yet exactly where it was stolen. Elko just happened to be the place where the Flyer's baggagemaster discovered that the body was missing."

"When did this happen?" Foxx asked.

"Today."

Foxx's head snapped around, and he asked, "That's the eastbound Flyer you're talking about?"

"Of course. The train you came on from San Francisco. By rights, I suppose it really ought to be your case, not mine."

"Go ahead, Griff," Foxx said when Presser paused. "Tell me everything you know about that missing body. Where was it shipped from, Sacramento or San Francisco?"

"San Francisco. It was consigned by the Dunkel Undertaking Parlor there to Henson and Son Undertakers in Kansas City."

"Why didn't the baggagemaster find out it was missing before the Flyer got all the way to Elko?" Foxx asked.

"That's the strangest part of the case. Whoever took the body left the coffin in the baggage car."

"I still want to know why the baggagemaster didn't find out sooner that the coffin was empty," Foxx said sharply.

"It seems the coffin was up against one side of the car, out of the way of the doors. The baggagemaster didn't need to move it until he had a big packing case to unload at Elko. That was when he found the coffin was empty."

"What kind of coffin was it?"

"A plain pine box, the kind they usually ship bodies in. Undertakers don't ship in fancy caskets, you know, they're afraid they'll get scarred up on the way. At least, that's what the undertaker in Elko told me when I asked him about the case."

"It was a full-sized coffin, I guess?"

"Yes."

"And was it completely empty when the baggagemaster opened it in Elko?"

"I just told you it was, Foxx. The body was gone."

"I'm not asking about the body. Was there anything at all in the coffin? Rags, paper, straw, anything at all?"

"Oh. There were a lot of rags. I guess they'd stuffed them down around the corpse to keep it from shifting."

"Was the coffin nailed shut?"

"No. The lid was screwed down."

"How many screws?"

"You can think of the damnedest questions to ask, Foxx!" Griff Presser frowned thoughtfully. "I didn't count them. There were six screws, I think. One at each corner, one on each side in the middle. No extra ones anyplace else, as I remember."

Maxine Bowden had listened silently while Foxx and Presser were discussing the train wreckings. Now she broke her silence for the first time.

"Are you thinking the same thing I am, Foxx?" she asked.

"I suppose so. I'd say we've found out why we didn't catch Jed Morgan in that trap we set in Sacramento. While we was out there looking for him to come out from under the train, he was in that coffin in the baggage car, laughing up his sleeve at us."

"I'd feel a lot more at home here if I had an idea what you and Miss Bowden were talking about," Presser told Foxx, a puzzled frown on his lean bronzed face. "I get the idea you know a lot more than I do about that stolen body, Foxx."

"If I do, it's because you just gave me the pieces to fit a puzzle together," Foxx replied. As concisely as he could, Foxx sketched for Presser the sequence of events that started at the Cliff House in San Francisco.

"Morgan must've seen that coffin loaded on the Flyer in Oakland," he concluded. "My guess is that he got the body out and dumped it in the river while the baggagemaster was helping the rest of the crew at the Carquinez crossing. It'd only take him a few minutes to unscrew the coffin lid, and an embalmed body would sink like lead. The train crews are always too busy to notice much during those ferry crossings."

"He wouldn't know where we were going, of course," Maxine said slowly, her voice a bit uncertain, as though her deductions were only a few seconds ahead of her words. "He probably got out of the coffin at Sacramento and saw us floundering around, trying to find him."

"That's right, Maxine," Foxx seconded. "I'd pulled the baggagemaster outa his car to help us try to trap him, so Morgan could've come out of the coffin without anybody seeing him."

"He wouldn't have known where we'd be getting off the Flyer, either," she added. "That's why he went on to Elko."

"I don't know how Morgan found out we weren't on the train any longer," Foxx said, frowning thoughtfully. "Unless the baggagemaster left his car at Elko, Griff. You remember anything like that happening?"

"Sure, I do. The baggagemaster needed help to get a big packing case out of the coach. He was in the baggage room at the depot there for quite a while, trying to find somebody who'd give him a hand."

"I'll bet dollars to doughnuts that when Morgan looked through the train and found we'd got off, he figured out it must've been at the last stop. Then all he had to do was buy a ticket on the first train west and get off here in Winnemucca. You wouldn't by any chance have noticed him, would you?"

"Maybe I did, at that," Presser said. "What does this Jed Morgan look like? I remember two passengers

getting on at Elko, and four who got off here in Winnemucca, but I didn't pay special attention to them."

"He'd be a hard one to miss," Foxx replied. "He's a
big man. Pushed-in nose, as I recall. He's half Kiowa.
Got a pockmarked face and an ugly mouth. Last time I
saw him was at his trial, back in Nebraska nearly five
years ago, but I'd know him."

"I'm pretty sure there was a man who'd fit that description on the train I came in on," Presser nodded.
"But as I said, I didn't realize that there might be a
wanted man on it."

"My God!" Maxine exclaimed. "He might be
watching us right this minute! I think I'll just stay
here in the car until we leave for Goldsburgh, Foxx."

"I don't blame you for feeling that way, but if Morgan's here, I want him to see you," Foxx told her.

"Of course. Just a little wishful thinking. I'll put the
red wig on when we go out. We will be going out,
won't we?"

"That's what I've got in mind. We'll have to go to
town anyhow, and in a little place like Winnemucca,
Morgan's sure to see you. He'll follow us, sure as night
follows day. Once we get him into open country, it'll
be a lot easier for Griff and me to take him." Foxx
turned to Presser. "What time does the haul start up to
Goldsburgh of an evening?"

"About six, at this time of the year. The district super wants the shipments to be delivered after the men
at the mines get to work. If they're too early, the trains
have to wait until the mine crews show up to unload
them."

"We'd better go into town and get our supper, then.
Griff, I suppose the Winnemucca stationmaster's still
got some of them '66 Winchesters that were shipped to

all these Nevada stations during that trouble with the Paiutes a few years ago?"

"I was thinking about those guns right this minute, Foxx. I didn't bring my rifle, and if I recall, you don't carry one with you. We can pick up one for each of us while we're in town."

"Don't get one for me," Maxine said. "I've never shot a rifle in my life, and I probably couldn't hit a barn door with one. I'll depend on the pistol I've got in my bag."

"But if we run into trouble—" Presser began.

Foxx cut him short. "Maxine's right, Griff. She ought not to be carrying a rifle. Remember, she's supposed to be a well-to-do young widow lady, Caleb Petersen's sister-in-law."

"Whatever you say," Presser shrugged. He glanced up at the nearest window. "If we're going to eat and pick up rifles at the depot before we go, we'd better get started pretty soon."

"Now's as good a time as any." Foxx turned to Maxine. "Now, I want you to stay in between me and Griff while we walk into town. Griff, we've got to keep our eyes peeled for Morgan. As far as I know, he hasn't got a rifle, so if he tries to get at Maxine, he'll have to get into pistol range. If he shows up, though, we'll try for him whether he makes a move or not."

Maxine had donned her red wig while Foxx and Presser were talking. Presser went out of the accommodation car first, and while Foxx stood in the doorway and scanned the landscape, Maxine squeezed past him and joined the Elko detective. Foxx stepped to the ground and moved up to join the others. Then, with the two men shielding Maxine as best they could with their bodies, the trio began walking toward the town.

If Morgan was watching them he made no effort to

attack. They got to the depot, went inside while Presser found the rifles and ammunition, and walked on down the street to the cafe, where they ate.

"I suppose the safest place for Miss Bowden to stay is in the accommodation car," Griff suggested as they were finishing their coffee. "I've already told the stationmaster to couple it into the string that's going up to Goldsburgh."

Foxx nodded through the smoke of the after-dinner stogie he was lighting. "We better get back to the car, then. If Morgan missed us while we were coming in, he'll be sure to see us on our way back."

Without appearing to do so, Foxx kept the street and the terrain between the town and the accommodation car under close observation while they made their way back. He'd made the mistake of underestimating his foe earlier, and had no intention of committing the error a second time.

There were literally dozens of hiding places from which the outlaw could be watching, though. Any of the gondola cars or boxcars that stood on the sidings would have provided shelter for him. So would the gullies that seamed the dry ground beyond the sidetrack on which the accommodation car stood. But Morgan, if he was indeed watching them, made himself as invisible this time as he had managed to do before.

At one end of the row of sidetracks a locomotive was chuffing back and forth, assembling the train that would soon be heading up the Bruneau River spur.

"Looks like we're right on time," Griff said. "We'll be rolling in another few minutes."

They got to the accommodation car and went inside. Maxine took off the red wig and the scarf that bound her hair and moved over to one of the windows; its bottom sill was just above her chin. She looked out and said over her shoulder, "There's sure not much to look at around here. Just bare ground and a bunch of gullies. I thought the West was full of trees and rivers and pretty scenery."

"Wait until we get across the flats," Griff Presser told her. "Once we begin climbing, you'll get all the scenery you want and maybe a little bit more."

Outside, the chuffing of the locomotive made itself heard and grew steadily louder. The accommodation car lurched slightly as it was coupled to the string that would form the train going up the Bruneau River spur. The car stood still for several minutes, then slowly began moving forward. Foxx moved to one of the chairs and sat down. Maxine left the window and settled on the divan. Griff Presser took the chair across the table from Foxx.

"How long will it take to get across the flats?" Maxine asked Griff.

"Oh, about two hours. As soon as we cross over into Idaho and start up through Duck Valley the scenery improves."

"I suppose all we've got to do now is wait again," Maxine said. "But I've learned one thing on this trip, Foxx. Detective work is the same everywhere: it's mostly waiting, whether it's in Chicago or out here in the desert."

"Or San Francisco and the mountains, or just about anyplace else," Foxx agreed. "Especially when you're trying to keep one jump ahead of a breed like Jed Morgan."

"How'd you happen to get crossways of him, Foxx?" Griff Presser asked. "You mentioned seeing Morgan at his trial, so he must be somebody you sent to prison a while back."

Foxx took his time answering. He uncorked the

bottle of Cyrus Noble and took a swallow, then lit a stogie. He was thinking back to the hour before sunrise on a midwinter day nearly six years ago.

A thin covering of fresh snow lay on the ground across the brushy hollow in the creekbed to which he'd tracked the Morgan gang after seven weeks of dogged pursuit. Sheer coincidence had resulted in the chase that was now at an end; Foxx had been able to take up the Morgan gang's trail only because he'd chanced to be a passenger on the C&K's transcontinental express when Blake Morgan's gang derailed the train on Christmas Eve.

Chance, too, had sent the early snow that had been the gang's undoing. Morgan and his motley crew had managed to stay ahead of Foxx until the weather changed, but he'd been close enough behind to pick up the hoofprints of their horses after the snowfall and track them to their hideout on the creekbed.

At the time of the holdup Foxx had been returning from a case that had taken him to Kansas City, the eastern terminus of the struggling new railroad. Like the other passengers he'd thought at first that the derailment was an accident. Then, when he'd made his way up the aisle of the tilted coach and dropped to the ground outside, he'd seen the gang of mounted men closing in and realized the derailment had been the prelude to a holdup.

There were seven men in the gang, and Foxx decided instantly that he'd be doing the C&K no real service by trying to stand them off single-handed. The locomotive boiler had exploded just as the gang closed in; the section of track Morgan's gang had ripped from the roadbed had been the last one before the engine started over the bridge on the North Platte River, and engine and tender had gone over the bank into the stream.

During the confusion that followed the boiler's explosion, Foxx clambered between two of the skewed passenger cars and took cover in the brush beside the tracks. He stayed hidden until the gang had completed its looting and started to ride off, then he managed to bring down one of the escaping outlaws with his revolver before walking back along the tracks to the little hamlet of Lewellen to organize a posse and pursue Morgan and his men.

It had been a long and frustrating chase, and along the way members of the posse had dropped out singly or in pairs. There were no lawmen among them; a few were storekeepers in Lewellen, the rest had ranches or farms in the vicinity, and all of them had personal business. As time passed that became of greater importance to them than trying to catch up with Morgan's elusive outlaws.

Foxx had gone on by himself. The lessons in reading trail-sign, taught him by his stern Comanche mentors during his youth, enabled him to stay on the track of the Morgan gang. He'd stayed on it even after the posse deserted him. Now, thanks to the snowfall, he'd at last come up with his quarry.

Crouched in the thin shelter of a winter-bare bush, Foxx watched and listened while Morgan and his men settled in for the night in their hideout. Overconfident after shaking off the posse, they set no lookouts. Foxx waited through the chilly night hours until the first shading of the false dawn showed. He picked his way carefully to the edge of the creek, moving noiselessly through the brittle brush.

He took his time and planned his shots carefully. The rifle he carried, an ancient five-shot Colt revolving *carbine, had been lent to him by one of the departing possemen, and Foxx had yet to fire it for the first time. The range was close, though, and when the light grew bright enough for shooting, he began firing methodically at his preselected targets. Foxx had no compunction about shooting the sleeping outlaws, just as they'd had no compunction about killing the two trainmen and four passengers in the derailment of the express.*

Five shots from the carbine accounted for four of the outlaws; though Foxx had no way of knowing it, one of the men he put out of action with those first rounds was Blake Morgan. By the time Foxx had emptied the Colt's five chambers, the three surviving renegades were firing back.

Foxx dropped to his belly when the carbine was empty and kept the remnants of the band under fire with his Smith & Wesson. He put a slug through Jed Morgan's thigh, shattering the bone, keeping Jed from escaping with the one outlaw who managed to get away by crawling to the rope corral and galloping off on a bareback horse when Foxx stopped to reload.

Both of the Morgans, father and son, stood trial for the train robbery and the killing of the trainmen and passengers. Blake, paralyzed by the slug that shattered his spine, was brought to the courtroom on a stretcher, and Jed hobbled in on crutches. The jury may have been influenced by their wounds, for Blake as the gang's leader drew a seven-year prison term, Jed was sent up for five. Foxx, made a celebrity by his pursuit and extinction of the gang, advanced quickly in the C&K's detective division, to become its head less than a year after the affray on the North Platte.

During the few instants required for him to swallow his drink and get his twisted stogie lit, Foxx's memory had flashed through the entire affair. Comfortable now, he answered Griff Presser's question.

"There's two Morgans, Blake and Jed. Blake's the daddy. I brought him and Jed in after they wrecked a C&K passenger train to rob it. Blake got shot up pretty bad, and it looks like Jed's out to make me pay for it."

"If I know you, he won't collect much," Presser smiled.

Maxine looked at Foxx and shook her head. She said, "After what's happened in this case, Foxx, I don't see how you can be so calm about the way Morgan keeps following us."

"Well, there's not much use in me raising a fuss," Foxx replied. "Sooner or later we'll catch up with Jed Morgan and that'll be the end of it."

CHAPTER 6

In the gray dawn Goldsburgh looked cold and unfriendly when Foxx and his companions got off the train. They walked silently, still stiff from a night of intermittent dozing and waking as the train creaked its way upslope to the town. On Goldsburgh's main street, which paralleled the C&K spur, only two lights showed, one from a saloon and the other from a restaurant. They wasted no time in heading for the latter.

They had the restaurant to themselves, though the dirty plates that stood on all but a few of the tables showed that they were not the first to come seeking breakfast. They began eating in silence, but the food and hot coffee began to revive them halfway through the meal.

"I guess there's a livery stable in here where we can rent horses, isn't there?" Foxx asked Presser. "Because I've got a hunch we're going to be covering a good deal of country before this is over with."

"Oh, Goldsburgh's a pretty fair-sized town, Foxx. It's bigger than Winnemucca. There's a livery stable here, all right. And a pretty fair hotel, too."

"Now that interests me a lot more than horses," Maxine said. "I don't know what you've got planned for us to do today, Foxx, but can we wait until we've had a bath and slept awhile to start doing it?"

"We're not in all that much of a hurry," Foxx told her. "I want to take a long ride alongside the spur, and talk to some of the mine operators, but I don't aim to start out till later. We'll sign in at the hotel, rest awhile and have our baths, then we'll start out."

"I hope they've got at least one docile horse at that livery stable," she said. "I haven't been in a saddle since I left the farm, and that's nearly ten years ago."

"I'd say you could stay at the hotel while Griff and me went looking, except for one thing," Foxx said.

"I know," she nodded. "I'm still being Vida Martin, and if Jed Morgan has followed us here, you want him to see me."

"That's about the size of it," Foxx agreed. "Morgan was smart enough to tail us from San Francisco, and I don't look for him to give up now."

"I think we're lucky if we can keep one jump ahead of him," Maxine said. "I'm beginning to understand what you told me about Kiowa Indians, Foxx. He's been somewhere close to us for almost a week now, and I still haven't set eyes on him."

"Maybe that's just as well," Presser said. "From what Foxx has told me, Morgan's too dangerous a man for us to let him get close."

"Oh, he's dangerous," Foxx agreed. "And the sooner we get hold of him, the better I'll feel about Maxine."

"So will Maxine," she said with a wry smile. "But right now I'll feel a lot better if I can get into a bathtub full of hot water and then crawl into bed for a little while."

An hour after noon, refreshed by sleep and hot baths, they set out on their rented horses. The sloping ground was sparsely wooded here. It was not forest land but foothill country, and everywhere they looked the ground was scarred by piles of dirt left when miners abandoned a worked-out claim or an exploratory shaft that had yielded no ore. Where there had been real strikes, the scarring was much worse, for in these places not only did the detritus of mining litter the mouths of the shafts, but the trees for as much as a mile in every direction had been cut to provide shoring timbers and fuel for the boilers of the oversized donkey-engines that powered the machinery.

Griff Presser had given Foxx the background information that he needed to decide which mines to call on and which to pass by; he wasted no time stopping at those owned by the syndicates, for he knew the local managers were little more than custodians and timekeepers, and had no real authority to make decisions. The men in their plush offices in Boise and Helena were the ones who wielded the real power.

Presser was familiar with the places where the C&K trains had been wrecked, and at each of these they stopped while Foxx studied the terrain and asked questions.

"If you're looking for a pattern, I don't think there is one," the Elko detective told Foxx as they scrambled around the site of one of the wrecks. "One time a rail was taken up, another time they put an old cogwheel across the tracks on the blind side of a bad curve, and the third time they just dragged a log across the tracks."

"Which might mean the wrecks was the work of three different outfits," Foxx said, as much to himself as to Presser, "or it might mean that the same bunch is responsible for all of them and they just used whatever was handiest."

"I think it's different outfits myself," Presser said. "It doesn't make sense to me that the syndicate would wreck a train hauling materials for a syndicate mine, or the other way around."

"How many times has syndicate freight been on one of the trains that got wrecked?"

"Only once. And one of the wrecks was an ore-train coming down to Winnemucca."

"You could be right, Griff," Foxx said. "There don't seem to be much of a pattern, at that." He squinted at the sun, now beginning to slant to the west, and went on, "It's time for us to head back toward town. It'll be dark by the time we get there, and I don't want to give Morgan a chance to bushwhack us and then get away because we can't see to chase him. We'll get an earlier start tomorrow and spend some time at the mines."

Their ride back in the fading light was uneventful. Leaving their horses at the livery stable, they walked the short distance to the hotel and started up the stairs. Their rooms were all on the second floor of the rambling frame building, and they reached Maxine's door first.

Taking her door-key from her purse, she turned to Foxx and asked, "Do you men want me to meet you at the restaurant so you can stop in at the saloon for a drink?"

"That might be a good idea," Foxx replied. "That bottle of Noble I've got in the room's just about a dead soldier now. I doubt there's a drink apiece left in it. Besides, I always like to stand at the bar in a saloon when I'm in a new town. You'd be surprised how much a man can pick up that way if he listens instead of flapping his jaws."

"I'll set my wig straight, wash my hands, and fluff up my clothes a bit, then," Maxine said. "And I'll look for you to be standing in front of the saloon when I pass by in about half an hour."

"On second thought, let's play it safe. I'll meet you here," Foxx answered. He started down the hall toward the room he and Presser shared, and had almost caught up with Presser when Maxine called him.

"Foxx, there's something wrong with the lock on this door. I can't get the key to turn. Will you see if you can get it open, please?"

Foxx went back and took the key out of the lock, examined it, and saw that it had no bends in the shaft and that the bit was properly aligned. He inserted the key again and turned it, but it resisted the pressure of his fingers. He rotated the key backward and tried again. This time the key turned, though not easily.

"That lock must need a drop of oil," Foxx told Maxine, handing the key back to her. "Better ask the desk clerk to take care of it when you leave."

"I hope I don't get locked in," she said.

"Well, maybe I'd better try the other side of the door."

Foxx took the key from Maxine's hand and turned the doorknob. The latch resisted. He increased the pressure and the latch released. He gave the door a push to open it.

With an odd-sounding metallic grating noise the door started to swing inward. Something in the sound and the movement telegraphed a warning to Foxx's fine-honed instincts.

He acted without an instant's hesitation. He and Maxine were standing close together, facing the doorway, and Foxx dove at the Pinkerton operative as though he were bulldozing a steer.

His shoulder caught Maxine just above the waist. The force of the dive carried both of them a yard or more down the narrow corridor, and their momentum flung them to the floor.

Before Foxx and Maxine landed on the worn hall runner, a shotgun's blast boomed. A cloud of smoke billowed into the hallway, and a volley of lead slugs spattered like vicious rain against the wall of the corridor across from the door.

CHAPTER 7

Stunned by the force of their fall, their ears ringing with the noise and concussion of the blast, Foxx and Maxine lay on the hall runner without moving. The acrid smell of gunpowder hung heavily in the air.

"My God!" Presser shouted from the door down the hall where he'd stopped to wait for Foxx. He ran back and bent over the prone forms of the pair. "Where were you hit?"

Foxx raised himself to a sitting position, but Maxine still lay stretched out on the carpet, gasping for breath.

"I wasn't," Foxx said.

"Are you sure?"

"I been shot once or twice. If I'd got hit, I'd know it."

"What about Maxine?"

"I—I'm all right," she gasped when she heard her name.

"All she needs is to lay still a minute," Foxx told Griff. "She just got the wind knocked out of her. I caught her a pretty good poke with my shoulder when I heard that set gun getting ready to go off."

"Was that what it was? A set gun?" Presser asked.

"That was it, all right. Ten- or twelve-gauge single-barrel, I'd say. Buckshot load, from the looks of them holes in the wall. We'll find out soon enough."

Voices were coming up the stairwell. Presser looked questioningly at Foxx. "Shall I try to keep anybody but the desk clerk from coming up here?"

"It'd be a good idea, Griff. It's a wonder everybody on this floor hasn't come noseying out to see what's happening."

"Regulars don't want second-floor rooms, so I imagine half the rooms on this floor are vacant. Whoever's in the ones that are rented are probably at the restaurant or the saloon. It's that time of day."

Presser went down to the landing to head off the curious.

Maxine was breathing more easily now. She tried to sit up, but did not quite make it. Foxx extended his hand. She grasped it and pulled herself upright.

"I owe you quite a lot, Foxx," she said. "If it hadn't been for you, I'd be hash meat now. Thank you isn't good enough, but that's all I can think of to say right this minute."

"It's plenty. I'm sorry I had to bang into you so hard, but I didn't have time to tell you to jump out of the way."

"You saved my life."

"Now, I don't want to hear any more talk about it," Foxx told her sternly. "Things like that go with the job."

"They never have before. If they do, your cases are a lot rougher than Allan Pinkerton's."

"Maybe he deals with a better grade of crooks."

From the stairwell Griff's voice could be heard, raised now in commanding tones. As Foxx got to his feet and helped Maxine to stand, the mutterings from that direction faded away, and in a moment Griff returned, followed by the desk clerk, a wiry little man wearing gold-rimmed spectacles.

"Oh, my!" the clerk said when he saw the splintered door and the pellet-holes in the wall of the corridor. "Somebody is going to have to pay for this damage!"

"I'll tell you what," Foxx suggested. "You find the man who put up that gun-trap in Miss Bowden's room and collect from him for messing up things."

"Now, Mr. Foxx, you know very well it's the law's job to find whoever's responsible for this!" the clerk sputtered.

"Then get your town marshal or constable busy."

"I can't do that. He's up in Boise, seeing a doctor."

"Me and Presser will do his job for him, then," Foxx told the clerk. "Unless you've got some objections?"

"Why—" For a moment the clerk debated silently with himself, then he said, "No objections at all, Mr. Foxx. I'm sure that the California & Kansas Railroad wouldn't be employing you gentlemen unless you were very well qualified."

"That's fine," Foxx nodded. "Now, suppose you help us by telling us a few things. First off, who come upstairs here while we was gone?"

"Why—nobody. Except the hotel guests, that is."

"You know all of them personal, I suppose?"

"Of course! There was Ed Blakemore, he's the chief mechanic at the New Home Mine. And Frank Carter, the works foreman for the Consolidated Mines. Then there was Otto Breyer and his partner, they own the Freestakes Mine. And—" The clerk frowned and said slowly, "There was a man by the name of Robert Brown, too. I—I don't know where he works. In fact, I never saw him here in Goldsburgh before."

"What'd this Brown look like?"

"Why, he was a big man. Not well dressed, but most

of our guests wear work clothes when they first come in."

"Tell me about Brown," Foxx said. "Did he have a pockmarked face?"

"Oh, he's a friend of yours, then," the clerk said, relief in his voice.

"I wouldn't exactly say he's a friend," Foxx told the man. "But I've got a pretty fair idea who he is. What time of day did he sign in?"

"About an hour after you people went out, as close as I can remember," the clerk replied.

"Did you see what kind of luggage he carried?"

"He didn't have any at all," the clerk said after a moment's thought. "He told me he'd left his saddlebags at the livery."

"And you didn't see him go out after he'd checked in?"

"Not that I can recall, Mr. Foxx."

Presser said, "If I remember, there's a back entrance to the upstairs floors. An outside stairway. Am I right?"

"Yes." The clerk hesitated for a moment. "Some of our more prominent patrons use it for privacy."

"Meaning they bring their lady friends in the back way?" Foxx suggested.

"We don't question our guests, Mr. Foxx," the clerk said primly. "As long as they pay their rent and are reasonably quiet, we try not to interfere."

"Sure," Foxx nodded. "That's a good way to run a hotel, I suppose, except when you rent a room to a killer. Now, you'd best get back to your desk. Oh—before you go, you better use your passkey and open up the room on the other side of the one me and Presser's in. We'll take care of moving the lady's luggage over into it. She sure can't stay in the one she's got, with the door all busted up the way it is."

For a moment the clerk wavered, indecision on his thin, pinched face. Then he smiled and said, "Whatever you say, Mr. Foxx. And I'll talk to the owner of the hotel tomorrow. I'm sure he'll see his way clear to paying for the damage."

"I'd imagine he will. It's his hotel," Foxx said.

When the clerk had gone, Foxx said to his companion, "Let's see what we can find out about that set gun. It might give us some idea about what to look out for later."

"Not more of the same thing, I hope!" Maxine exclaimed.

"I hope not too. But with a man like Jed Morgan it's hard to be sure."

Foxx went into the room, followed by Maxine and Presser. A double-barreled shotgun, its barrel sawed off to a stub little more than a foot long, had been wired to a chair and aimed at the door. From the inside doorknob a length of stout wire extended to the back of the chair. The end of the wire had been pushed through the slats of the chair's back before being looped around both of the gun's triggers. When the door was opened widely enough, its swing would take the slack out of the wire, the loop would be yanked back and pull both triggers at once.

"It's simple enough," Presser commented as they examined the device. "How'd you catch on to the setup, Foxx?"

"I heard the wire scraping along the back of the chair. And the door had a funny feel to it, I guess that's what I noticed first. But I'd already started swinging the door open and I didn't see how I could get hold of it in time to stop the wire from pulling tight."

"I'm glad you've got good ears," Maxine said. "I don't think I'd have noticed the door feeling funny or heard the wire scraping, either. It was just luck that my key jammed."

"It wasn't all luck," Foxx told her. "Morgan had to've been in a hurry. He didn't know how long we'd be away. I'd say he messed up the lock when he picked it. Had to force it a little bit, maybe."

Presser pointed to the shiny rims of the gun's sawed-off barrels. "Look how bright those saw-marks are on the muzzle. That was done just a few hours ago. He must've decided to set that trap as soon as he got here."

"He doesn't waste any time, does he?" Maxine said.

"No, and we can't waste any, either," Foxx cautioned them. "What we'd better do right now is to get you moved, then all of us go to supper together. We'll come back up here after we eat, and figure out how we're going to handle things tomorrow."

"I don't think there's much use looking any further, Griff," Foxx told his Elko detective as they sat at a table in the Hardrock Saloon. On the wall above the bar the hands of the cased pendulum clock were creeping toward noon, and they'd been trying since early morning to get on Jed Morgan's trail.

Their only problem had been that Morgan seemed to have left no trail at all. The train on which Foxx and his companions had come to Goldsburgh had long since returned to Winnemucca, so there was no way they could ask the crew whether an unauthorized passenger had been seen dodging away from one of the empty gondola cars that had made up almost half the manifest. At Goldsburgh's two restaurants the cooks and waiters had shrugged and looked blank when given Morgan's description, and when prodded by questioning had said they couldn't be expected to remember the faces of everybody they served. In the saloons the barkeeps had responded in much the same fashion.

There were two places in Goldsburgh that sold guns, a hardware store and a general merchandise store. Neither of them had sold a double-barrel twelve-gauge shotgun, or any shells for such a gun, during the past month. The only horses the liveryman had rented had been the three hired by Foxx for the inspection trip he and Presser and Maxine had taken on the previous day.

"Morgan's a lot smarter now than he was when I sent him to the pen," Foxx said, pouring himself a fresh drink and pushing the bottle of Cyrus Noble across the table to Presser. "Looks like he made good use of all them years he was locked up."

"I've heard crooks say that there's no school like a prison," the young detective replied. "And I guess they were right, because your man's as slippery a customer as I've ever run across."

"Morgan or no Morgan, I've still got to do the job I was sent up here for, Griff. I don't aim to leave Maxine by herself, though. She'd be all right in a city, I suppose, but out here she's pretty much a fish on a sandpile. I want you to stick around town after we eat, keep an eye on her while I get on with my work."

"Why can't we all three go, like we did yesterday?"

Foxx shook his head. "I can cover more ground by myself, for one thing. And I don't want to have to be worrying about Morgan dogging along after us while I've got my mind on trying to put a stop to this fight that's building up between the syndicates and the little mine operators."

"That's a pretty big order. Both sides are about to boil over. Wrecking our trains to cut off supplies has been all that either side's done so far, but I'm sure that what I told you about the syndicates building up a gang of hardcases is true."

"I never doubted that for a minute. Big companies have done that all over the country. Suppose it is true, Griff. When do you think the syndicate bosses will give the word to start?"

"I'd hate to try to guess, but I don't think the day is too far off."

"That's why I've got to get moving. It's easier to stop a thing like this before it starts than it is after there's been men hurt, maybe killed, on both sides."

"It's going to mean moving fast," Presser warned. "The time's real close when they're going to start butting heads."

"I could tell that from the way the small operators were talking yesterday. And the C&K will be hurt a lot worse than losing some cars in a few wrecks if this fuss boils up into a real all-out fight."

"I don't know how much luck you can expect to have, Foxx. The little men might listen to you, but the syndicates are just too big."

"Their size don't scare me one bit, Griff. When push comes to shove, the big syndicates know they'd lose a lot more than the little fellows if I tell them the C&K won't haul any more freight for either side until they've settled their differences."

"I don't see how that can be the case. The syndicates have a hell of a lot more money than the small operators."

"From what Jim Flaherty told me when he was lay-

ing out this job in San Francisco, Caleb and his front-
office men have found out that the syndicates are
mostly operating on borrowed money. They'd be paying interest on millions of dollars with nothing at all
coming in if we quit hauling their ore."

"Now, that makes sense. Just so I'll know, Foxx,
what're you planning to do?"

"Backtrack over part of the ground we covered yesterday. Talk to the small miners, see if they'll listen. I
remember the places you showed me where I need to
stop, so I ought not have too much trouble."

"No. All you've got to do is keep close to the spur."

"And all you've got to do is keep an eye on Maxine
and see that Jed Morgan don't hurt her. It might even
be a good idea for you to go down to the livery stable
later and get your rifle if you two decide to go for a
walk or something."

"I'm afraid it'd take more than an invitation from
me to get that young lady out of the hotel," Griff
grinned. "But I will pick up my rifle, just in case."

With a metallic whirr the clock above the bar started
striking. Foxx glanced at it and said, "If I'm going to
cover any ground, I'd better get started. I'll stop at the
store and get some jerky so I can eat while I ride. You
and Maxine can eat whenever you've a mind to."

There were a half-dozen customers waiting at the
general store when Foxx went in, and only one clerk,
who was trying to serve all of them. Foxx stood behind
the row that lined the counter, waiting for someone to
leave and make room for him. The harried clerk was
doing the best he could, but the patrons were getting
impatient.

At last a woman who'd been filling a huge market
basket turned to go, and the clerk looked at the man
who'd been standing next to her. Both of the next two

men in line were standing with their backs to Foxx.
The first one was tall and rangy; he wore wrinkled
black trousers, their cuffs frayed, and a checked flannel
shirt. His long hair, black streaked with gray, hung
down his back to his shoulders.

Next to him stood a broad-shouldered, burly man;
his sweat-stained tan poplin shirt was tucked into the
blue denim jeans that marked him as a miner, for they
bore the leather waistpatch showing they'd been made
by Levi's in San Francisco. Before the clerk could ask
the thin man for his order, the burly man shoved the
first one aside.

"Damn it, Charley!" the big man growled. "I got to
be back at work in twenty minutes! You can take your
turn after I get my tobacco and fixings."

"Was here first," the other said. "Big hurry. Want to
buy cheese and crackers."

Only after he'd heard the man speak did Foxx realize that the man first in line was an Indian. He said
nothing, but when the miner put a foot behind the Indian's ankle and gave him a shove that sent him
sprawling, then drew back a booted foot to kick the
prone man, Foxx's sense of justice was outraged. He
stepped up to the miner.

"What the hell you think you're doing?" the miner
growled.

"You can wait your turn, mister, just like the rest of
us," Foxx said levelly. "It won't take but a minute for
the clerk to wait on the fellow ahead of you."

"It ain't any of your business!" the miner snapped.
"Damn redskin scum hadn't oughta be waited on before a white man!"

"He had if he was here first."

"What the hell! You're one of them softheaded

Indian-lovers! Well, we don't need your kind around here!"

Without warning, the miner started a roundhouse swing, his fist coming up from thigh-level toward Foxx's jaw. Foxx drew his head back just enough to let the blow swing past him; the man's clenched fist hit the brim of Foxx's hat and knocked it off. While the miner's arm was still rising, Foxx grabbed his wrist in both hands, made a quick half-turn, and brought the arm down on his own shoulder.

In the same smooth motion that he'd learned to use while wrestling with Comanche youths his own age, Foxx swiveled his torso and bent forward. Using his shoulder as a fulcrum and the miner's arm as a lever, he tossed the big man to the floor a half-dozen feet away. The miner landed with a thud that knocked the breath out of him for a moment. Panting, drawing deep breaths, he came to his feet.

"You need to be taught manners, you Indian-loving son of a bitch!" he snarled, his hand flashing toward the gun belted at his waist.

Foxx's S&W was out of its cross-draw holster while the miner's hand was still inches away from his own gun butt. The miner stopped his effort to draw and stood frozen-still, his eyes on the unwavering muzzle of the long-barreled pistol in Foxx's hand.

"You just lost your place in line unless you feel like taking it away from me," Foxx told him, his voice low but icy.

For a moment the miner's hand trembled and flexed, inches away from his gun butt. Then with a snort of anger mingled with disgust, he turned and stamped out of the store. Foxx looked for the Indian, to tell him to go ahead and place his order, but the thin man had vanished. Holstering his gun, Foxx faced the clerk and the remaining three customers, who'd stood motionless during the brief fracas.

"Looks like I lost a couple of customers for you," he apologized to the clerk. "Not that they was about to buy a lot."

"That's all right, mister," the clerk replied nervously. "If you got an order, I'll be glad to fill it for you now."

"No need, son," Foxx said calmly. "These other folks was here before I was. You go ahead and tend to them. I'll get in line and wait my turn."

When Foxx left the store, carrying a sack containing jerky, parched corn, a chunk of crumbly Cheddar cheese, and a quarter-pound of soda crackers, he looked around for the Indian, but the man was nowhere to be seen. With a shrug Foxx walked on down the rutted dirt street to the livery stable and asked for the horse and saddle he'd rented the day before.

While he waited for the horse to be saddled, Foxx reclaimed one of the '66 Winchesters that he and Presser had left in the storage closet provided by the stable for customers' long guns. When the stableboy finally led his animal around, Foxx slid the rifle into its saddle holster, dropped the sack of food into the saddlebags, and rode out of town in the direction Griff Presser had led them the day before.

He was just lifting the reins to turn the horse onto the narrower road that led to the C&K spur, when a man leaped from the brush bordering the road and landed directly in front of the animal.

Foxx reacted by instinct. He swept his revolver out, and his finger was on the trigger before he saw that the man was the Indian called Charley. The Indian stood his ground unflinchingly despite the menace of the pistol in Foxx's hand. Somewhat sheepishly, Foxx holstered the gun.

"You come damn close to getting a hole in your belly!" he said sharply. "Why in hell didn't you yell at me before you jumped out in front of me?"

Charley shrugged. "Not know name."

"My name's Foxx, and I work for the C&K railroad. Now, you mind telling me why you give me enough of a start so my back hair's still standing on end?"

"Want to thank you."

"You don't need to thank me, Charley. I didn't do a thing, except what I thought was right."

"*Na* Charley," the man said. "*Pah-na-sha.*"

"Indian name?"

Nodding, the man repeated, "*Pah-na-sha.*"

Foxx remembered that the Comanches looked on the Shoshones as distant relatives. Though their languages differed in many respects, they came from the same Utean root-tongue. He tried to summon enough Comanche to reply, but he had forgotten too much of the language he'd learned and spoken for so many years of his youth during the adoption forced on him by the Kotsoteka Comanches.

Foxx said the man's name after him, then shook his head. He said, "*Na Comanche, Pah-na-sha.*"

"*Na Comanche. Shoshone.*" Pah-na-sha looked at Foxx narrowly and at some length, then said glumly, "*A-ye-ha! Na Comanche! Foxx tei-e-ka!*"

"That's right, Pah-na-sha, I'm white. Not even a little bit of The People's blood in me, far's I know."

"How you learn?"

Foxx made a quick decision; usually he was reticent about his Comanche upbringing, but this time an exception seemed to be in order. He said, "I was brought up by the Kotsotekas. Just a little while after I got my grown-up name, I left 'em. That was a long time ago, and I've just about forgot the language."

"You not forget *che-to-kee*."

Foxx thought for a moment, then half guessed. "Good manners?" he asked. Pah-na-sha nodded vigorously. Foxx went on, "Good manners is the same anyplace, and it don't matter what color your skin is."

Pah-na-sha shook his head. "When is Shoshone, white men forget. Not all. Some good, more bad."

"I guess you're right, at that." Belatedly, Foxx remembered the cheese and crackers he'd bought. He pulled the sack out of his saddlebag, dumped the jerky and parched corn into his coat pocket, and handed the bag to the Shoshone. "Here. This is what you went in the store for."

Pah-na-sha looked in the bag, looked up at Foxx for a moment, and then extended his hand, still holding the sack. "No. This your food."

"I got that jerky and corn you just seen me put in my pocket. That's all I need. You take that and welcome."

Gravely, Pah-na-sha nodded. "To you I say thank you, Foxx. I do not forget."

"I'd stay and talk awhile, Pah-na-sha, but I got business up ahead. Maybe we'll run into each other again, before I leave Goldsburgh."

"Maybe. Peace go with you, Foxx."

Foxx lifted a hand to acknowledge Pah-na-sha's farewell and toed the horse ahead. He reached the spur and turned south. The trail beside the spur was little used at this point, and Foxx had to ride slowly. He had gone only a short distance when he heard the shooting begin.

A single shot sounded, somewhere ahead. Another

followed it after a moment's silence, then another. Soon the reports swelled into a small volley.

Foxx nudged the horse's flank with his toe, and the animal began to gallop. The firing ahead continued, increasing in intensity.

CHAPTER 8

Foxx slid the Winchester out of its saddle scabbard as he drew closer to the shooting. From the close spacing of the individual gunshots, he guessed that at least a half-dozen men and perhaps as many as eight were involved in the fighting. He was reasonably sure that his estimate was correct. Just as a soldier in combat learns to distinguish between the reports of enemy weapons and those of his own force, Foxx could identify the characteristic sounds of different rifles. He'd recognized the sharp, cracking reports of three or four modern rifles, Winchesters or Remingtons, and the deeper-toned muzzle blasts from two heavier-caliber weapons, Sharps or old army Springfields, and at intervals he'd been able to make out the flat booming of a large-bore shotgun as well as the short, angry barking of one or two Colt revolvers.

Foxx's ears told him when to rein in, tether his horse, and move ahead on foot. The previous day's scouting trip was still fresh in his mind; he recalled that a short distance ahead on the trail, between where he now stood and the C&K spur, there was a small independent mine. As Foxx advanced he entered an area where the miners had cleared away all the trees for shoring and fuel, and what low-growing underbrush remained was thin. He slowed down, dodging from one sparse patch of cover to the next, until he was close enough to see the low-lying mine buildings—offices, sleeping quarters, and machine sheds—and beyond them the tall rectangular frame structure that housed the hoist. Foxx reached an unusually thick clump of brush and stopped to take stock of the situation.

By now the firing had become ragged. The few scattered shots that still sounded came from behind the little cluster of buildings at the head of the mine shaft. A shot rang out close at hand, to Foxx's right, and the spurt of smoke from its muzzle blast gave Foxx the position of the sniper.

Foxx stopped for a moment, debating the best move for him to make. The sniper close at hand tempted him, but judging from the sounds of the firing, he'd help the miners more by adding his firepower to those who were defending the other side of the mine buildings. He looked ahead and saw that by mounting a small ridge that rose beyond the mine shaft, he could reach the far side of the slope beyond the buildings with his rifle fire.

Foxx started for the ridge, but had gone only a few steps when his ears caught the faint whisper of footsteps behind him. Foxx whirled, his rifle leveled. Pahna-sha was hunkered down beside a bush a dozen yards behind him. The tall, thin Shoshone had an ancient Whitneyville Colt in one hand and in his other the sack of cheese and crackers that Foxx had given him. He looked up at Foxx, a smile on his lined face.

"Pah-na-sha!" Foxx exclaimed in a low angry whisper. "Damn it, this is twice today I've damn near shot you by mistake! What the devil are you doing here?"

"Hear shooting, think maybe you need help. Come to see." He held up the old Colt. "Bring gun."

Foxx looked at the Shoshone and his outdated

weapon. "Where in the hell did you get that thing?
You didn't have it when I seen you back there a
ways."

"Hide pistol in brush before go to town. Don't take
there ever. *Tei-e-ka* don't like Indians have guns."

"Well, I thank you for coming to help me, Pah-na-
sha, but I ain't sure what you can do. Or what I can
do, for that matter."

"You help men in mine?"

"That's what I was figuring to do."

"Good." Pah-na-sha pointed the Colt to the spot
where the attacking rifleman was located. "Good. We
kill that one first, then go shoot others."

"Now, hold on! I ain't sure I want to go killing anybody, just yet. I'm trying to stop the killing, not do
more of it."

Pah-na-sha grunted sourly. "You don't fight
Shoshone way. We see enemy, we kill him. Then don't
be enemy no more."

Pah-na-sha's logic struck home. Foxx realized that
the Indian's offer to help might tip the scales in favor
of the miners more quickly than he could hope to do
so alone.

"All right, Pah-na-sha. You go on over to where
that lone sniper's working. I'll go up that ridge and see
what I can do to discourage his friends."

Pah-na-sha nodded. "Big coup for you, kill all three.
Maybe you fight like Shoshone after all."

"We'll talk about coups after we see how we come
out. Now, let's see if we can give them fellows inside
that mine a little help."

Still holding the sack of cheese and crackers in his
left hand, Pah-na-sha began worming his way toward
the rifleman in the gully. Foxx watched him for a

moment, then started for the ridge he'd chosen as his vantage point.

With his flank covered, Foxx felt free to move fast. Leaving the Shoshone to attend to the lone attacker, he ran at a crouch up the ridge. When he reached the highest point in the crest, Foxx could see over the low roofs of all mine buildings except the hoist, and was situated at an angle that gave him a wide field of fire.

He watched the next rider dash in. The attackers were hitting the mine Indian-fashion. One at a time they galloped toward the buildings until they came within range, letting off a quick shot or two as their mounts turned in a short arc. The paths of their horses as the attackers veered away took them into an area along the side of the buildings on which the defenders could not bring their rifles to bear.

Foxx waited on the crest of the ridge for the next rider to make his sortie. He followed the attacker in his sights until he saw the horse beginning to turn, then let off a shot from the Winchester. The animal reared, and in spite of the distance between them Foxx heard the animal's high-pitched whinny of pain.

Digging his heels into the beast's flanks, the rider managed to stay in the saddle, but the horse's gyrations made accurate shooting impossible. Foxx fired, but his slug missed and kicked up a puff of dust behind the dancing horse. The shots alerted the rider, though. He galloped away at a zigzag, and as he rode Foxx could hear the man's warning shout in the suddenly quiet air of the early afternoon.

"Hold back. They got a man outside and he's flanking us!" the retreating rider called.

Foxx located the other attackers when they replied to the warning. They were in a hollow beyond the mine buildings, hopelessly out of range.

"How in hell did they work that?" one of them shouted in reply.

"Damned if I know! But we got to figure another way to get at 'em or give it up for now!"

"Let's call it off!" came the reply. "Blunt said all we was out to do is warn 'em!"

"Suits me! What about Costa?"

"You follow us, Lefty! We'll yell at Costa as we go past!"

Foxx saw that by cutting across the angle of the course the attackers would have to take to get past the mine buildings, he might be able to get in a parting shot. He started down the flank of the ridge, taking giant running strides, but before he'd spanned half the distance he needed to bring him within range, the three horsemen were sweeping past the hoist and speeding their horses to a gallop. He looked for Pah-na-sha, but the Shoshone was nowhere in sight.

Thudding hoofbeats warned him that the attackers were making their getaway. The three riders swept past the corner of the mine buildings. They galloped to within a few yards of the gully where the lone rifleman was sheltered, and one of the men reined in while the other two kept going.

"Costa!" called the man who'd halted. "Mount up and come along!"

Without showing himself, the man called Costa asked, "What's happened? Are we pulling out?"

"Damned right we are!" the rider replied. "The bastards got a man outside someways and now there ain't no way to get at 'em. We ain't done here, though! Soon as we get our whole bunch put together, we'll come back and burn 'em out!"

Now Foxx saw the man in the dry wash for the first time, as he scrambled up to level ground and began running toward a rock outcrop beyond the gully. Foxx raised his Winchester, but even before he'd gotten the gun shouldered, he decided not to shoot. He decided quickly that to bring down one of the attackers would do nothing but bring his companions back, and he saw no point in prolonging today's fight. There'd be time to deal with the gang later, at a place and time of his own choosing.

Standing motionless on the ridge to avoid drawing the gang's attention, he watched the man from the gully disappear behind an outcrop. A few moments later he came out on the outcrop's opposite side, mounted now, and spurring to catch up with the others, who'd already vanished around a curve in the trail.

Foxx started down the embankment, and before he'd reached the flat, Pah-na-sha came walking slowly toward him.

"We not fast enough," the Shoshone said, unhappiness in his voice. He held up his old Colt. "And gun no good. Shoot, but no bullet. Powder old."

"We were as fast as we could be. And I saw what I was interested in, Pah-na-sha. You got any idea who them riders were?"

Pah-na-sha shrugged. "Bunch outlaws. Not from here."

"You wouldn't know where they're camped, would you?"

"No. Can find easy, if know country."

"Which I don't. If you was me, where'd you start looking?"

Pah-na-sha pointed to the southeast. "Badlands. Is where outlaws go hide."

"You know your way around out there, I guess."

"I know, Foxx. To Shoshone is home."

"How'd you like to find out for me where that bunch

has made camp, Pah-na-sha. I'll pay you for your work, of course."

"Easy to find. Follow tracks. But from you I take no pay, Foxx."

"I can't ask you to work for me for nothing, damn it." Foxx looked at the Whitneyville Colt dangling from the Shoshone's hand and remembered that the gun had failed to fire. He said, "I'll tell you what, though. If you'll find where them fellows have got their camp, I'll give you a new .44 Colt and a box or two of shells."

Pah-na-sha's face brightened. "You take me when you go to kill them, too?"

Foxx hesitated. He suspected that in a fight with the renegades, Pah-na-sha might prove to be a little more enthusiastic than would be really necessary. However, if the Shoshone was to guide him to the outlaw camp, there'd be no way to keep him from taking part in the fighting that was almost sure to follow.

"All right, Pah-na-sha. You'll be with us if there's any fighting to be done. Have we got a deal?"

"We got deal. I start now."

"Wait a minute! I ain't in all that much of a hurry. You go on and prowl around, but don't let 'em catch on you've spotted their camp. Then you come to the hotel in Goldsburgh and tell me where it's located. If I ain't around, you find my man, his name's Griff Presser, and he'll know where to find me."

"Griff Presser," Pah-na-sha repeated. "I will do this thing as you say, Foxx."

"Good. When you got the camp spotted, you and me will see what kind of scheme we can come up with to take care of 'em."

"Only one way to take care of outlaws, Foxx. Kill them."

"Damned if you don't sound like the white men who say the only good Indian's a dead one. But find the camp first, and you and me can settle the rest after that."

Foxx watched while Pah-na-sha started off, the Whitneyville Colt still dangling from his right hand. For a moment Foxx was tempted to call him back and offer to get him a better gun, in case he ran into trouble while scouting. Then he decided there was no use tempting fate, and set out for the mine building.

As a precaution Foxx took out his handkerchief and knotted an end of it onto the barrel of his rifle before he got too near the mine buildings. He walked slowly, holding the rifle up and swinging it from side to side. Fifty yards from the low barnlike structure that bore the sign "Office," a man's voice called, "You better hold it right there, mister, till we find out who in hell you are and what you got on your mind!"

"My name's Foxx. I'm the chief of detectives for the C&K Railroad, and all I want to do is talk."

"How do we know you're who you say you are?"

"I'll be glad to show you my badge, if that'll help."

"Hell, any ragtag-bobtail shitass can get him a badge!"

"That's about all I got to offer," Foxx said. "Except if you're wondering why them fellows that jumped your mine rode off in such a hurry, it's because I was shooting at 'em from out here while you was holding 'em off from inside."

A second voice said, "See there, Big Joe! I told you I heard shots that didn't come from them renegades' guns!"

Foxx called, "That was me you heard shooting. I don't guess you could see me from inside there, because I was off at one corner of your building, covering the places you couldn't."

"That's what you'd say if you was out to trick us! Go on, get on your way, mister! We're grown-up men, we can take care of ourselves without no help from you!"

"Damn it, Big Joe, let the man come in!" the second voice said angrily. "If he ain't who he says, we can handle him!"

"All right, Little Joe, if that's how you want it," the first voice said. "But remember you're to blame if he comes in here shooting." The heavy timbered door under the sign "Office" swung open. "Come on in."

Foxx covered the rest of the distance to the building and went inside. The light was dim, since all the building's windows had been boarded with inch-thick planks. He stood just inside the door for a moment while his eyes adjusted to the changed light. As his vision cleared, he could make out the two men standing in front of him.

One was a full head taller than Foxx and twice as broad. He wore miner's boots and Levi's denim jeans and was shirtless, his upper torso clad only in a knit union suit that clung to his massive chest. His arms bulged with biceps as big as Foxx's upper thighs. The second man was half the size of the first; he looked like an adolescent youth beside the big man. His head came just above Foxx's shoulder, his waist was smaller in diameter than the big man's forearms, and his thin, almost rectangular head perched on a spindling neck.

"I'm Joe Farnum," he said, extending his hand. "Little Joe, to just about everybody. This grouchy bastard here's my partner, Joe Bailey."

"Big Joe," Bailey said.

"I told you my name. Foxx. If you want to see my badge—"

Big Joe and Little Joe spoke at the same time, one saying "Yes," the other, "No." Foxx took out his wallet and showed them the gold badge engraved with his name that was pinned inside the fold.

"I guess you're who you said you are, all right," Big Joe admitted grudgingly. "But you can't blame us for being suspicious, Foxx. This fight that's started has been blowing up for quite a while, and it's got us a mite jumpy."

"I don't blame you," Foxx told the big man. "Who was it shooting at you a while ago?"

"Damned if we know," Little Joe said. "It ain't like we wasn't warned. The Boise syndicate's been trying to buy us out for a year now, and the Helena syndicate's been after us just about that long."

"And you've turned them down?" Foxx asked.

"You're damned right we have!" Big Joe snapped. "The Two Joes Mine is all we got, and maybe it ain't much, but we aim to keep it."

"If we can," Little Joe added.

"We can, by God!" his partner snapped.

"I get the idea the syndicates have been squeezing you men pretty hard," Foxx said.

"Both of 'em have told us we'd better make up our minds to sell, or else," Big Joe volunteered.

Foxx took out one of his twisted stogies and lit it. "Are you men the only independents that's had a syndicate offer?"

Big Joe snorted. "We ain't found an independent miner yet that the syndicates ain't after. Sometimes it's the Boise bunch, sometimes the outfit from Helena."

"How many of the other independents have been told 'or else'?" Foxx asked.

"We wouldn't know about that, Foxx," the big man answered. "It ain't rightly our business, you understand, to go asking questions."

"Have any of them besides you been shot at?"

This time it was Little Joe who answered. "Not that we've heard about. There sure has been a lot of 'em sell out and move on, though."

"How many?"

"There used to be about thirty of us, between here and the Snake. There's less'n twenty now. Of course, a few of 'em quit because their lodes petered out."

"What would you call a few, Little Joe?"

"Four or five."

"That's half," Foxx frowned. "And did the rest of them sell to the syndicates?"

"Six did that I know of. The syndicate lawyers can do a hell of a lot of persuading, Foxx. They don't have to come right out and say anything, you know. They just hint around, but anybody with a grain of sense knows what they're talking about."

"And I got a feeling it's going to get worse before it gets better," Big Joe put in. He spat toward a corner of the room. "I guess it's safe to take a drink now, with them rascals gone." He walked over to the table that stood in the center of the room and picked up the blue-glazed jug that stood on it. He offered the jug to Foxx, saying, "This ain't fancy liquor, Foxx, but it goes down all right."

Foxx took a swallow from the jug. He kept himself from gasping, puffed furiously on his stogie, and waited for the top of his head to settle back in place before asking, "After this business today, are you going to change your mind and sell out?"

"Foxx, there ain't a syndicate or anything else that's going to change our mind as long as we got our guns and plenty of ammunition for 'em," Little Joe said soberly.

"How many of the other independent mine owners feel that way?" Foxx asked, looking from one of the partners to the other.

"Now, that's a hard question to answer," the small man replied, frowning thoughtfully. "I know we ain't the only ones that's turned down the syndicates, but I wouldn't like to guess how many of them's going to keep on saying no after they been treated to a little dose of hot lead."

"There's maybe ten or twelve that's set in their minds the way we are," Big Joe volunteered.

"Set enough to fight back?"

"Most of 'em. Why?" the big man asked. "And why's your railroad so all-fired interested, anyhow?"

"I'd think you could see that, Big Joe," Foxx told him. "The C&K's got to have enough customers to make our freight hauls pay off."

"Even if all the mines was owned by the syndicates, they'd still have to ship on your railroad," the big miner pointed out. "You'd haul the same amount of freight."

"We would as long as we're the only railroad up here, but the UP's building a loop that'll cut across this part of the country," Foxx explained. "If there's only syndicate freight to be hauled, the syndicates can play us off against the UP and the UP against us. First thing we knew, we'd be losing money."

"I guess that makes sense," Big Joe nodded.

"We're interested in keeping things the way they are now," Foxx went on. "That's why we're trying to help you men fight the syndicates, whether they're from Boise or Helena."

"How're you going to fight 'em?" Little Joe asked.

"They're not leaving us any more choice than they are you," Foxx told the pair. "Not if they're bringing in a bunch of gunmen to try and force you to sell out."

"What you're saying is, when they start shooting, you aim to shoot back," Big Joe frowned.

"Just like you're doing," Foxx reminded him.

"And you want to join up with us?" Little Joe asked.

"That's the general idea."

"Well, you got off to a good start, just a little while ago. As far as I'm concerned, we'll take the railroad's help and be glad to get it," the small partner said.

Foxx asked the key question now. "Suppose all you independents got together and made a deal to help each other fight the syndicates, no matter what it took," Foxx suggested. "Would you go along?"

"Hell, if all the others did, we'd just about have to," the big man frowned.

"Somebody's got to start a deal like that moving," Foxx reminded them. "I'll do what I can, but your miner friends are going to listen to you a lot quicker than they would to me. They'd figure I'm just trying to get 'em to pull the C&K's chestnuts out of the fire."

Big Joe nodded slowly. "I'd sure feel that way, if you hadn't jumped in to help us today, without waiting to be asked."

"Damn it, Big, let's go along with Foxx's scheme!" Little Joe said to his partner. "We sure can't lose nothing."

"I guess not." Big Joe turned to Foxx. "All right. We're in. When do we start shooting?"

"Not right this minute," Foxx told him. "If we can settle this without gunplay, we'll all be better off. Give me a few days, to see if I can get to somebody who might stop the shooting before it gets started."

"Damned if I know who that'd be," Big Joe frowned.

"Well, I do," Foxx said. "It'll take a few days to find out about, though. You men just sit tight until I get back."

"Mind telling us what you got in mind?" Little Joe asked.

"Not a bit. I'm going up to Boise and see if we can get the governor of the Territory to move over onto our side of the fence instead of the syndicates'."

CHAPTER 9

"You're going where?" Griff Presser asked, his jaw dropping as he stared at Foxx across the barroom table.

"To Boise City," Foxx repeated, then added, "to talk to the governor."

"What're you planning to do, have him call out the militia?" Maxine asked.

"I don't think they've even got a militia here, Maxine," Foxx replied. "Even if they have, the C&K's just an outside business as far as Idaho Territory's concerned."

"What do you have in mind, then?" she persisted.

"I'm going to see if I can get the governor to tell the mining syndicates to pull in their horns. He's about the only one I can think of that might be able to talk turkey to them."

Presser's moment of surprise had passed. He asked with a thoughtful frown, "Even supposing he can, do you think he will?"

"It's hard to say, Griff. I don't know a thing about him, not even his name. I ain't about to guess what he'll say or do. He's the head man in the Territory, though. It's his job to keep things peaceful."

"If you don't know what he'll do, why bother, then? Why don't we just go ahead and let the two Joes get the independent miners together and tackle the job?

From what I've seen of miners, they run pretty tough. They ought to be able to handle any hardcases the syndicates send to intimidate them."

"Suppose the other miners don't go along?"

"Then we'd be right where we are now, I guess," Presser said after a momentary hesitation.

"That's what I been thinking," Foxx said. "But even if we do get the miners together, that's going to mean a lot of shooting. If the governor stops the syndicates from pushing the independents out, there won't be no fighting."

"But the fighting's already started, hasn't it?" Maxine asked. "I got the idea those men out at the Joes' mine today weren't just shooting blank cartridges."

"None of us was, Maxine. But nobody got hurt, either. And I've found out that once blood's been spilt, there ain't no way to mop it up without leaving a dirty place. I figure it's worth a try to keep things from busting wide open."

"I guess it is, at that," Presser agreed. "Well, Maxine and I will be here to keep an eye on things while you're gone."

"You'll be doing that by yourself, Griff. Maxine's going with me. As long as she's not here, we won't be worried about Jed Morgan getting another chance to kill her."

"What's going to keep him from following you to Boise City if Maxine goes along?"

"I've got it figured out so that Morgan won't tumble onto us being gone in time to find out where we are, let alone catch up with us."

"How do you plan to do that?" Maxine asked.

"I got this fool idea about going to Boise City while I was still out at the mine, so I asked the Joes the quickest way to get there. They told me there's a stage stop up at the Snake River crossing, and that ain't but a little ways from here. The stage'll get us there in about six hours."

"You're still thinking about Jed Morgan being after me, aren't you, Foxx?" Maxine asked.

"He don't strike me as being a man that gives up, once he's started something."

Presser repeated the question he'd asked earlier. "What makes you think he won't trail you from here to Boise City?"

"We'll have to ride out of Goldsburgh about four o'clock in the morning to make connections with the stage," Foxx replied. "Morgan ain't likely to be watching at that time of day."

"I don't mind getting up at four o'clock," Maxine said. "But I don't mind staying here, either, if I'm going to be in your way. I'm sure Griff can handle Morgan if he should try again."

"You ain't going to be a bit of a bother," Foxx told her. "Anyhow, after that close shave you had with the set gun, it'll rest your nerves a little bit if you can just forget about Jed Morgan for a day or two."

"Whatever you say," Maxine told Foxx. "I'll admit, it will be nice to walk down the street without that feeling that he might be watching me."

"I figured you'd see it that way." Foxx turned to Presser. "Now, Griff, there's a few things you need to be doing while I'm gone. We'll talk about them after we go up to our room, then I'll leave everything to you until I get back from Boise City."

When the trio returned to the hotel, Pah-na-sha was sitting on the edge of the board sidewalk, waiting. He looked at Foxx's companions for a moment, and started to walk away.

"Hold on, Pah-na-sha," Foxx said. "If you got something to tell me, go ahead."

"I tell you by yourself," the Shoshone replied. "Not talk in front of woman. They flap mouth too much."

Dropping his voice, Foxx told Maxine, "You wait inside for us. It'll be easier to do that than to try to change a Shoshone's mind."

When Maxine was out of earshot, Pah-na-sha said, "Place you look for out in badlands, like I say."

"You found it, then?"

"Easy. They not try to hide tracks."

"Where's the hideout, Pah-na-sha?"

"Hard to tell, you not know landmarks."

"Well, is it north or east or south or west of the Joes' mine where we had that brush with them today?"

"East. In coulee."

"How far east?"

"Maybe—" Pah-na-sha stopped and shook his head. "No can tell, Foxx. Come on, we go there."

"Damn it, Pah-na-sha, I can't go right now. Anyway, I'm not ready to start fighting just yet."

"They fight you, fight your friends," the Shoshone pointed out. "They enemies, Foxx. Best thing you do, kill enemy quick, before he kill you."

Foxx shook his head. "I can't go with you right now, and that's all there is to it."

"We go tomorrow, then?"

"No. It's going to be a while yet."

"Maybe a while too late."

"I imagine they'll still be there when it's time for us to go after them," Foxx assured Pah-na-sha. "You didn't let them see you while you was scouting their camp?"

"They not see, all right."

"How many was there?"

Pah-na-sha held up eight fingers.

"That's about two more'n I'd figured," Foxx frowned.

"Now is best time we go," Pah-na-sha urged again. "They all asleep, we kill easy."

"Taking care of them hardcases is going to have to be put off two or three days," Foxx told Pah-na-sha. "I've got to be someplace else that long. But you keep an eye on the place, will you? If it looks like they're getting ready to go after another mine, hightail back to town and tell this man here. He'll know what to do."

"You sure we no go now?" Pah-na-sha asked, making no effort to hide his disappointment.

"I'm sure. Don't worry, though. I'll have that gun I promised you when I get back, and you ain't going to be left out when we get around to taking care of that bunch."

"I wait, then."

"How'll I find you when I get back?" Foxx asked.

"Not worry, Foxx. I find you."

Foxx watched Pah-na-sha's back as the old Indian walked away. He said to Presser, "I don't imagine you'll need a man for anything, the little time we'll be gone, Griff, but I'd trust that Shoshone as far as I'd trust any man. Now, let's get on upstairs and do what figuring we need to. I got a feeling that four o'clock's going to get here before I'm ready for it."

Late in the afternoon Foxx and Maxine stepped off the dusty stage onto an equally dusty street in front of the Boise City stagecoach station. The mining boom that had started a few years earlier was having its effect on Idaho's territorial capital. Wooden business buildings were being replaced by more imposing structures of brick, and the streets were crowded with drays and wagons.

"This is a pretty good size town," Foxx remarked as he and the Pinkerton operative walked down the street toward the hotel to which the stage agent had directed them.

Maxine looked at the unpaved streets, the board sidewalks, and the mixture of frame and brick buildings. "I suppose so. It's hard to get used to small towns, though, when you live in a place like Chicago."

"Oh, it sure ain't Chicago, or San Francisco, either. But you got to admit it's a cut above Goldsburgh and Winnemucca."

"Right now I'm less interested in Boise City than I am in resting up from the jolting we got in that stagecoach. All I can think about is taking a bath, and maybe napping awhile before dinner. If you don't mind, that's what I'll do while you tend to whatever business you planned on."

"It's a little bit late for me to start today. Tomorrow'll be plenty of time. You have your bath and rest."

"Foxx. Can I leave off this wig while we're here? I've had to look like somebody else for such a long time that I'd sort of like to be myself for a day or two."

"Why, sure. There's no reason to put it on until we get back to where Morgan's going to see you."

"Thanks. That'll make me feel a lot better. What did you want me to do tomorrow?"

"I didn't bring you here to work, Maxine. I just didn't think it was a good idea to leave you back in Goldsburgh with nobody but Griff to keep an eye on you."

"But if you're going to be busy with the governor—"

"That won't take more'n tomorrow. We'll be on our

way back the next day, and all I aim to do in what's left of today is find out where the capitol is and who the governor is; anybody I talk to can tell me that. What few questions I need to ask today, I can get answered while I'm having a drink to wash the dust outa my gullet. Then I'll have a bath and maybe forty winks and we'll have supper together."

"That sounds more like a vacation than a business trip."

"We can spare a little time to rest. Now I'll get the name of a good restaurant, one where we can get something besides fried steak and potatoes. We'll have a late supper, and then we can both get a good night's sleep without having to keep one eye open looking for Jed Morgan."

"I'll look around the stores tomorrow, then," Maxine said, her voice almost gay. "Maybe I can find a few things I'm running short of. I didn't plan on being out in the field this long, so I traveled a little bit too light."

"You'll have plenty of time to poke around by yourself tomorrow. Likely I'll have to wait awhile before I can get in to see the governor," Foxx said. He pointed to a three-story building on the street just ahead. "There's the Overland Hotel sign. We'll register, then I'll do some noseying around. Does seven o'clock strike you as a good time to eat supper?"

"It strikes me just fine, Foxx. Our rooms will probably be close together, so tap on my door at seven, and I'll be ready."

Their rooms were not only close together, they adjoined. Foxx went to the washstand, poured some water from the pitcher into the big bowl and washed his hands and face quickly to get rid of the road grime, then went downstairs to the hotel's barbershop for a shave before stepping into the barroom that opened off the lobby. A drink of Cyrus Noble took the first layer of dust off his throat, and the second bourbon, which he sipped after lighting a stogie, removed the rest.

Waiting until the barkeep stopped in front of him to refill his glass, Foxx said, "When you've finished that, pour yourself one on me."

"Thanks, but it's a little early. If it's all the same to you, though, I'd enjoy a good cigar."

"Help yourself."

After he'd had a sip from his freshly filled glass, he asked the barkeep, "You'd know the name of the governor of Idaho Territory, wouldn't you?"

"Let's see," the man replied, wrinkling his forehead to show he was thinking. "The real governor just got voted in to go back to Washington, to Congress. Seems to me the new man's a lawyer, name of Barnes, if I recall rightly."

"Thanks. Now, how do I get to the capitol building from the hotel here?"

"Friend, there ain't no such building in Boise City."

"This is the capital of the territory, ain't it?"

"Sure. But nobody's got around to putting up buildings to show it is."

"Seems I remember that a territory's got to have a legislature and tax collectors and somebody to keep books. They'd have to have a place to work in."

"Mister, they do what anybody else would, rent whatever rooms that's vacant in buildings around town. Why, the legislature met right here in the hotel the last time it had a session."

"Sounds to me like a hell of a way to run things."

"Maybe so. But I guess it suits 'em, or they'd change it."

"One more thing," Foxx said. "What's the best place to eat here in town?"

"You can't do much better than the hotel restaurant if you want good American cooking. Most of the cafés are run by Basques and Italians and some Canucks that've come south lately."

"Canucks are Frenchmen from Canada, ain't they?"

"That's right. If you've got a taste for the kind of food they dish up, you might try the Canadian café. Just walk up Fort Street until you see the sign."

"Thanks. Now I'll take a bottle of that Cyrus Noble to carry up to my room and stop pestering you with questions."

At that hour of the day the men's bathroom on the floor was deserted. Foxx soaked luxuriously in the six-foot-long porcelain tub and, after returning to his room, stretched out on the bed and thought about the arguments he could offer the governor if he succeeded in getting an interview the following day. Before too long, he fell asleep.

Dusk had already begun to dim the room when Foxx woke up. He was reaching for his vest to get a stogie from the pocket when he remembered his dinner arrangement with Maxine. A glance at the Pailliard Repeater told him that he'd have to hurry if he was to be on time. Dressing hastily, Foxx tapped at the door of the adjoining room right on the stroke of seven.

When Maxine opened the door, Foxx stared at her as though he were seeing her for the first time. With the red wig on she'd seemed pale and faded, and the strain of being a target had kept her face tight and anxious most of the time. Now her face was radiant. Her blond hair was fluffed into a high bun; without the red wig her eyebrows and lashes looked darker, better suited to her light brown eyes. With a discreet touch of lip rouge emphasizing her full lips, Maxine's appearance had been transformed.

"Looks like that rest helped a lot," he told her.

"It did. I feel like myself again. I'm hungry as a bear, though. I hope you found out about a good café."

"We got two choices, plain American food at the restaurant here in the hotel, or a French place the barkeep told me about."

"You said you didn't want fried steak," she reminded him. "That's what we'd probably get downstairs. If it's all the same to you, let's try the French restaurant."

They dined quite adequately at the Café Canadien, on pâté de fois gras and sauced eggs *mollet,* followed by grilled stream-fresh trout with drawn butter, served with potatoes Anna. Out of deference to his dinner companion, Foxx ordered champagne. They finished one bottle with the first course and without asking, the waiter opened another to go with the trout.

Foxx and Maxine were too interested in the food to interrupt their dinner with conversation. Maxine scooped up the last of the raspberry sherbet that had been their dessert and pushed the empty bowl aside.

"That's the best meal I've had since I left Chicago," she sighed.

"I was about to say the same thing, except I'd've made it San Francisco," Foxx told her.

"We were too busy and worried the little time I was there for me to pay attention to what I ate. Of course, it's that way half the time I'm at home, especially when I'm on a case."

"What kind of work do you do for Pinkerton, Maxine?"

"Business cases, generally. Office embezzlements, forgery, things of that sort. Your friend Romy Dehon gets the criminal cases, but I suppose as soon as I've been there long enough, I'll get some of them too."

"Romy's the one that really got Allan Pinkerton started hiring woman operatives, I guess. Of course, he used women spies when he was running the Secret Service, during the war."

"We don't see each other very often, even though we both work out of Pinkerton's main office. But I guess you know how that is."

"Romy's a good operative; she knows her business," Foxx said, then added, quickly, "Of course, you do, too, Maxine."

"I'm glad you think so. There are times when I'm not really sure."

"Don't worry, you do. Like I promised, I'll put that in a letter to your boss after we close this case." Foxx lit a fresh stogie, then drained his coffee cup and said, "Well, unless you want some more coffee, we might as well go."

They walked slowly along the board sidewalk up Fort Street, heading for the hotel. The night was young and the streets busy, with a surprisingly large number of blue-uniformed soldiers in the crowds. Foxx noticed that most of them seemed to be moving from one saloon to another, not a hard thing to do, since there seemed to be a saloon on every corner.

As they drew closer to the center of town the crowds grew thicker. Two or three times Foxx had to step quickly in front of Maxine to keep a drunken, roughly dressed miner or a reeling soldier from bumping into her.

"I'm glad I'm with you and not by myself," Maxine said after the third such incident. "This place is rougher than Chicago's First Ward! If you don't know Chicago, the First Ward is a slum where women don't dare go out on the streets alone after dark."

"But what happens when you've got to go into a rough neighborhood on a case?"

Maxine shrugged. "I carry my pistol in a purse and a blackjack up my sleeve and hope I don't have to use either one."

"Have you had to?"

"Only twice. The blackjack, not the pistol. My husband taught me how to use both of them, before he died."

"How long has he been dead?" Foxx asked, then said quickly, "I'm sorry. I guess that's a question I ought not have asked."

"It doesn't bother me now," Maxine replied. "He died three years ago. I moped around for two years, then decided I was being a fool to try to live in the past. Allan had offered me a job right after Bob died, so I went down to his office and told him that if his offer still stood, I was ready to go to work."

"So you really haven't been in the business a long time."

"No. But I think I'll stay with it, now that I've started."

They'd reached the hotel now. They walked together through the almost deserted lobby and up the stair. Foxx waited at the door to Maxine's room while she took the key out of her purse and unlocked the door.

"You don't have to worry about looking for me tomorrow," he told her. "Take the day for yourself. I oughta be back here at the hotel by suppertime, and our stage back to Goldsburgh leaves at six the next morning, so unless something happens that'd make us stay over another day, we'll eat supper earlier than we did this evening."

"That's fine, Foxx. I'll see you tomorrow afternoon, then. And thank you for such a nice evening."

"I enjoyed it as much as you did. I'll see you tomorrow, then."

In his own room, Foxx slipped the Cloverleaf Colt revolver out of its sewn-in pouch-holster and laid the gun on the dresser. He was on his second drink, and the stogie had burned down to an unsmokable butt when a grating of metal on metal broke the silence.

Instinctively Foxx glanced at the door leading to the corridor, and the thought flashed through his mind that somehow Jed Morgan had managed to trail him and Maxine to Boise City. He stepped to the dresser and was picking up the Cloverleaf when the door between his room and Maxine's swung open.

Maxine stood there, her hair unbound and cascading over her shoulders. The light from her room streamed through the loose web of hair, turning it to bright gold. It also streamed through the almost transparent fabric of her nightgown and silhouetted the contours of her body.

"I thought," she said, stopped and started over, "I wanted— Well, it's been such a lovely evening, Foxx, that I just hated to see it end. I hope you don't mind."

CHAPTER 10

"Why, I don't mind a bit, Maxine."

Maxine stepped in and closed the connecting door. She looked around the room, then stepped back, and for a moment Foxx thought she was going to leave. Foxx put the Cloverleaf Colt back on the dresser and gestured to the easy chair. Maxine sat down, perching on the very edge of the seat, and he could tell that her composure was hanging by a thread.

"Wouldn't you like a drink?" he asked. "It won't be champagne or gin, but if you don't mind bourbon—"

"Bourbon's fine. With just a little water in it, please."

Foxx fixed her drink and poured for himself. He looked at the two straight chairs in the room and decided to sit on the bed.

Maxine said hesitantly, "I thought about unlocking that door for quite a while before I did it, Foxx. I know you and Vida Martin are—"

"Wait a minute," he broke in. "I'll tell you the straight truth about me and Vida. She's pretty much in the same boat you are. She's a widow and her husband's only been dead a couple of years. Now, me and Vida think an awful lot of each other, but when I'm away from San Francisco, which is most of the time, she does what she wants to, and so do I. And she don't ask any questions of me when I get back, and I don't ask her what she's been up to while I was away. Does that make you feel any better?"

"Yes. Yes, it does. Quite a lot. I didn't understand how things stood between you and her, but I didn't want to—"

Foxx finished for her, "You didn't want to come between us."

"Something like that." Maxine had almost finished her drink during Foxx's explanation; now she drained the glass and put it back on the table. She went on, "You know, when a woman's been used to having a man around, it's not easy for her to get along without one."

Foxx could see that Maxine had run out of courage. He stood up and went over to the easy chair, sat down on its padded arm, and leaned over to bring his face on a level with hers.

Maxine turned her face up to Foxx's, and their lips met. She opened her mouth and Foxx felt her tongue on his lips, a soft, tentative touch. He met her halfway, and suddenly Maxine's mouth came to life. She slid a hand between the buttons of his shirt, her fingers entwined in the curly hair on his chest. Foxx's hands went to Maxine's shoulders, then gently slipped down to caress her breasts.

Maxine shivered as Foxx's fingertips brushed her nipples, which extended with desire. She broke away from their kiss long enough to say, "It's a long time now since I've been with a man."

"Then we better not wait," he said. He stood up and stepped out of his trousers, and let his partly unbuttoned shirt slip down to the floor. He began to unbutton his linen undersuit.

"Wait," she said suddenly. "Let me."

Foxx stopped. Maxine came up to him and quickly

finished the unbuttoning, then after a momentary hesitation, stripped off the garment. Foxx moved to her and took her in his arms. They kissed, and while their lips were glued together, Maxine's hand slid down and closed around his swelling erection. She gasped, a long deep inhalation, and her free hand joined the one that had touched him first.

Foxx slipped the loose neck of Maxine's garment over her shoulders. She shrugged out of the straps that held the gown up, and it fell to her waist. Foxx pushed it over her hips and it slid to the floor.

When their naked bodies came together, Maxine began to moan. When Foxx made no move to take her, Maxine spread her thighs and guided his erection between them. She clasped her thighs together and rocked her hips, pressing firmly down on him. Without warning she began to jerk her hips convulsively, and Foxx could feel the warmth of her juices spreading over him.

"Oh, damn!" Maxine half sobbed. "I didn't want to do that!"

Foxx was still motionless, his arms around Maxine's torso, crushing her breasts to his chest. "Why get so upset?" he asked. "It didn't hurt anything that you was in a hurry. We've got all night. Come on, now, let's go get in bed."

"It's just that I've been thinking about you all day, and when I could feel you between my legs, I—well, I just couldn't help letting go."

Foxx closed her mouth with his. After a few moments he broke their kiss and started to brush his lips over her breasts. Then he took one soft, pink nipple into his mouth, and began running the tip of his tongue around its base.

"Oh, God, that feels good!" Maxine gasped. "But I

want you inside me now, Foxx! I'm just burning up inside!"

Leaving her breasts, Foxx sought her mouth with his own, and slowly he let himself down on her body, his erection between them, pressing on Maxine's soft belly.

Foxx raised his hips and Maxine's hand darted down to grasp him. He did not thrust into her quickly but moved slowly and deliberately, yet even before he'd entered her fully, she was gasping in another quick orgasm.

Maxine's small moans and sighs died away, but Foxx stayed in her and kept thrusting slowly. After she'd lain silently for a few moments, she opened her eyes and said, "I just need to talk a minute, to get my mind off what's happening to me when you drive into me."

"Talk all you want to. It won't bother me a bit. If you want me to stop—"

"No, no!" she exclaimed quickly. "You're giving me what I've needed for a long time." For several minutes Maxine lay quietly, her eyes veiled, enjoying Foxx's long unhurried strokes. Then she opened her eyes and asked, "Why is it that I'm so aroused by you? I go out with men in Chicago, not often, but when I've got an evening free. Most of them try to get me in bed, and I'd really like to sleep with some of them, but when it comes to the point of saying yes, I just can't."

"I never have figured out what it is between a woman and a man that gets them in bed together," Foxx told her. "I don't suppose anybody ever will."

"Whatever it is, I'm glad it's working for us." After another brief silence she asked him, "Are you getting too tired to go on?"

"Not yet. You said you didn't want me to stop, so I've been holding back."

"I still don't want you to stop." Maxine closed her eyes, a blissful smile on her lips. She groaned with delight each time Foxx thrust into her, and only a few moments passed before she was going into her spasm again, her hips rising almost involuntarily to meet Foxx's increasingly vigorous strokes. When at last the tremors stopped shaking her, she lay utterly limp, her eyes closed, her lips parted in a smile.

Foxx was beginning to wonder how long Maxine could go on and how long he could continue to hold himself back, when she opened her eyes and looked up at him.

"I'm being selfish, Foxx. And you're being wonderful. Are you tired out by now?"

"I can keep going a while yet," Foxx told her.

"Let me get on top, then. I've always wanted to, but you're the first man I've ever felt like asking. Do you mind?"

"Whatever you want to do suits me. Only, I can't hold back as good as I can when I'm on top."

"Let's go, then. You've waited long enough."

They rolled over, reversing their positions without Foxx withdrawing, and Maxine looked down on him, her eyes wide. She began swinging her hips from side to side, her oscillating motions growing faster and faster. Foxx reached up and cupped her swaying breasts, stroking their pink tips with his thumb.

Maxine released a long ululating cry and pressed down on Foxx's groin; then she was shaking and jerking out of control again in a prolonged spasm this time, and in the midst of her uncontrolled release Foxx let himself go, jetting fiercely, his body's tension flowing and subsiding in a series of muscle-tightening jerks that did not stop until Maxine had lurched forward, her breasts covering his face, the perfume she wore mingled with the musky aroma of a woman who has been completely satisfied.

"Oh, Foxx!" she sighed, her voice a soft, throaty murmur. "You don't know what you've done for me! I've never had sensations like that before!"

"I feel pretty good right now myself," Foxx told her.

"I never knew how different it would feel with me on top. What else haven't I learned yet?"

"Oh, I imagine there's a few things. And we've got the whole night ahead of us to see how you like them."

"I want to try everything, Foxx!" Maxine said, sitting up and stroking his chest and the rippled wall of muscle that covered his flat belly. "Let's make the most of every minute we've got!" She leaned her head on Foxx's shoulder and whispered, "You'll never know how glad I am that I finally got up enough courage to unlock that door!"

Foxx had not started out until the morning was well along, but as he walked down Fort Street toward Sixth, he reminded himself of the office hours kept by most of the attorneys he knew, and decided that an earlier start would have been time wasted.

He and Maxine had breakfasted in his room, and nine o'clock had come and gone before he'd managed to get away. At the desk he'd stopped and asked for the address of Jonathan Barnes's law office, and strolled down Fort Street to Sixth. He turned the corner and saw the building the desk clerk had described, a new two-story brick structure. Barnes's name was on a neatly lettered sign, gold on a black background.

Foxx went in. A hall ran the length of the building; a sign on the first door repeated the legend borne by the one outside, and invited visitors to enter. He opened the door into a large room, lined with shelves filled with books bound in brown buckram. Beyond the antechamber he could see a second room, where a man sat at a rolltop desk, studying a sheaf of papers. He looked up when Foxx stepped into the anteroom.

"Were you looking for someone?" he called.

"I'm looking for Governor Barnes."

"Well, I'm Barnes, but I'm not the governor. Not yet."

Foxx stopped short, frowning. He asked, "Did I knock on the wrong door? Is there another Mr. Barnes in Boise City?"

"No. I'm the man you want, but my title's purely temporary, and so far it's just honorary." When he saw that Foxx did not understand, he said, "Come in, Mr.—"

"Foxx. Chief of the detective division of the California & Kansas Railroad, out of San Francisco."

"Mr. Foxx," Barnes nodded. "I'm familiar with your railroad, though it doesn't enter Idaho Territory yet."

"Our main line doesn't, Governor. We've got a couple of spurs that run up into the mining country south of the Snake."

"So you have. I'd forgotten that." For the first time Barnes seemed to be aware that Foxx was still standing. He indicated a chair that stood near the corner of his desk.

Barnes was a small man. Even seated, Foxx's eyes were on a level six or eight inches higher than the lawyer's. Barnes had a thin New England nose, a narrow jaw, and lips set in a firm straight line. His eyes were a washed-out blue, deep-set below sparse brows. His hair, cut unfashionably short, was thin and receding badly.

Foxx broke the silence that had settled over the room after he sat down. He said, "I guess I'm a little mixed up, Mr. Barnes, about whether or not you're the governor. Would you mind setting me straight about that?"

"What I was trying to convey is that I hold the title of Acting Governor. The previous governor has been elected as the Territory's delegate to Congress, and until a formal replacement is named by the President of these United States, the title I have is without any meaning, Mr. Foxx. Power of action is at present vested only in the Territorial Legislature, which meets twice yearly. As acting governor I can do nothing more than sign bills passed by—and initiated by, I might add—the legislature. In short, Mr. Foxx, Idaho Territory has a governor in name only at present, and this is the situation, I'm afraid, that will prevail until, as chief executive of our nation, the President decides he's ready to appoint a bona fide governor."

After he'd waded through Barnes's explanation, Foxx asked, "I take what you said to mean that you're just keeping a chair warm for whoever the President finally decides to make the real governor?"

"You put it very aptly, if a bit inelegantly. I perform a number of meaningless routine and ceremonial jobs, but I have no power to initiate any actions that would result in decisions that could be enforced by an exercise of power."

"That is to say, you can sign papers and make speeches, but you can't do much of anything else?"

"Succinctly stated. What did you come to ask for, Mr. Foxx? A job? A new road? Authorization to establish a township?" Barnes shook his head. "Of course not, you said you're representing the California & Kansas Railroad. That must mean the road has plans to lay tracks in this territory. If that is indeed the case, then you seek one of two things—a subsidy, or use of the executive power in exercising the right of eminent domain to secure rights of way for your tracks. I'm sorry to disappoint you, Mr. Foxx. None of the actions I've named is within my power to perform."

"You keep getting ahead of me, Gov—Mr. Barnes. I don't want those things."

"Oh? What did you come looking for, then?"

"Somebody who can stop a war that's about to break out over in the mining country east of here."

"A war?" Barnes's domed head snapped up, and he stared at Foxx with a frown. "That's a strong word, Mr. Foxx. Perhaps you'd better explain."

"That won't take long," Foxx said. "I got an idea you'd know a lot more'n I do about your own territory, so I can skip over everything else and get right down to business."

"I'm reasonably familiar with my home territory, Mr. Foxx," Barnes said dryly. "I know that the mining syndicates based here in Boise City and the Daly syndicate from Montana Territory have been trying to buy out the independent operators in that section, and I'm aware there have been some disagreements between the independents and the two syndicates. Is that what you refer to as a war?"

"No, sir. I'm talking about a real bang-up shooting war, with a bunch of outlaws and hardcases sent in by the syndicates to run the independents off."

Barnes frowned and asked, "You're talking about large-scale violence, then, Mr. Foxx?"

"I don't see how you could call it anything else. There's already been some shooting, and there's going to be a whole lot more."

"Do you have any legal evidence that either of the syndicates actually hired these men and ordered them to attack the independent miners?" Barnes asked thoughtfully.

"No, sir. It could be either one of 'em. Or it could be that the Boise City bunch and the Daly bunch have got together and are working in cahoots."

"What's the California & Kansas Railroad's interest in this, Mr. Foxx? You certainly don't expect me to believe that your employers are simply being altruistic."

"If you mean we figure to get some good out of keeping a war from starting between the independents and the syndicates, we do. We spent a pile of money building them two spurs up into Idaho Territory to haul ore and mining machinery. There won't be much business for the C&K if there's a fight going on."

"I see. It is quite obvious when you put it that way, though I'll admit the thought hadn't occurred to me. Well, what do you expect me to do?"

"Why, stop it, before a lot of men get killed."

"And how do you propose I stop it?"

"You got a lot of soldiers out at that fort on the edge of town. Send some of them over to the mines to keep the peace."

"Unfortunately, as I've already explained, my authority as acting governor doesn't extend that far."

"You can still talk, can't you, Mr. Barnes?"

Barnes frowned. "I don't seem to follow you, Mr. Foxx."

"What I'm getting at is, in this job you got you're bound to be pretty well acquainted with some of the big men that's behind the mining syndicate here in Boise City."

"Quite well, even if they do go directly to Washington with their requests. In fact, I have been told that if I show myself to be amenable to their desires, they will exercise their not inconsiderable influence to secure the office of governor for me."

"Since you said a minute ago that you ain't really the governor, I got an idea you turned down their deal?"

"Mr. Foxx, I am not a politician. I also have some principles that most politicians do not seem to share. I believe that no public office should be filled on the basis of private barter. To be quite specific, I have made it clear that my name is not for sale, and that if by any unforeseen circumstances the President should appoint me governor, the syndicates will get no special consideration."

"Well, that does you credit, Mr. Barnes, but it seems to me that if the Boise City syndicate can get you the job, they can keep you from getting it, too."

"They have mentioned that to me during the course of our infrequent conversations," Barnes said dryly.

Foxx went on, "I guess you got pretty much the same offer from the Daly syndicate's men?"

"Certainly. Marcus Daly's representatives have used the same tactics that the local syndicate has employed."

"And you told the Daly bunch the same thing?"

"Precisely. Quite frankly, Mr. Foxx, I am resigned to the fact that there is no possible set of circumstances under which the President will appoint me, when he does get around to filling the governor's chair. And I have a very strong suspicion that one of the reasons he has delayed for such a long time in making an appointment is because the local syndicate is pressing him to name the man they want to fill the office, and the Daly syndicate is exercising an equal amount of influence trying to have their candidate selected."

"Which sorta leaves you out in the cold with no place to go."

"You phrase it correctly, Mr. Foxx."

"And you don't think you could jawbone?"

"I beg your pardon?"

"You don't feel like you could get these Boise City men and the Daly syndicate men together here in your office and persuade them to call off their gunslingers?"

"Oh, come now, Mr. Foxx! We're living in a civilized age! I can't imagine the syndicates resorting to violence! There are legal ways for them to achieve their objectives."

"Maybe they figure doing it legal would take too long," Foxx suggested.

"I find that hard to—" Barnes stopped suddenly. "Are you very sure of your facts, Mr. Foxx? Are they based on firsthand observation, or merely suspicion?"

"Well, day before yesterday I got mixed up in a shoot-out between some syndicate gunmen and a couple of independent miners the syndicate men were trying to run off. I guess that's about as firsthand as you can get."

"You can prove that the gunmen were employees of one of the syndicates?"

"No, sir. I can't prove it, even if I know it's a fact."

Barnes sat silently for several moments, his eyes focused on the shelves of lawbooks that lined his office as well as the adjacent room. Finally he said, "I'm afraid I can't help you, Mr. Foxx. Even if I had the authority to act, I'd want to justify any action I might take with proof that would stand up in court."

Foxx had been fighting a sense of failure from the beginning of his conversation with the acting governor. He stood up.

"Thanks for your time, Mr. Barnes." He looked

around at the law books lining the two rooms. "It just seems to me like you could find some legal way in them books to stop men from getting killed in a fight that ain't legal. It looks to me like we're getting to where laws ain't much account unless there's men around who'll make 'em work the way they was supposed to. And I ain't talking about lawyers and courts and judges. I won't take up no more of your time, Mr. Barnes."

CHAPTER 11

"So, it's up to us to take care of that bunch of syndicate hardcases," Foxx concluded. He and Griff Presser were sitting at the table in the Hardrock Saloon that they'd come to consider their office. A bottle of Cyrus Noble stood on the table between them. Foxx went on, "If Barnes wasn't lying to me, about all he's got is a fancy title, and since he told me that before he heard my story, I guess he was telling the truth."

Foxx and Maxine had gotten back to Goldsburgh the preceding evening. Both of them were badly in need of sleep after their strenuous activities in bed during their final night in Boise City, and Foxx had put off telling Presser of his disappointing conference with the acting governor until the next day.

"Well, I've had a little bit better luck than you did," the young detective said. "The two Joes took me with them when they went out to talk to the independent miners. Some of them backed off, but not all of them. We'll have a few men going with us if we take on the syndicate's gunmen."

"I don't think it's a question of 'if,' Griff, but more like a matter of 'when.' What'd you call a few?"

"Five or six, counting the Joes. Then there'll be you and me. It's not much of an edge, but at least we won't be outnumbered. And there's Pah-na-sha. I suppose he'll be along, but I don't know how much good he'll be, old as he is."

"Don't ever misjudge a Shoshone, Griff. They're fighters."

"I haven't seen him yet, by the way," Presser said.

"Maybe that's because he didn't want you to see him. He'll be showing up, soon as he finds out I'm back."

"How's he going to find out?"

"He'll learn about it somehow, you wait and see." Foxx lit a stogie and poured a bit more whiskey into his glass. After he'd swallowed it, he asked Presser, "I don't suppose you've seen Jed Morgan skulking around?"

"No, but even if he has been, I don't think I'd have seen anything. Morgan's too slick a customer to leave any sign."

"He's cagey, but sooner or later he's going to push his luck too far. Then we'll have him."

"What's our first move going to be, then?" Presser asked.

"Just about what you'd expect. But before we can make it, we've got to get Pah-na-sha to show us where that hideout is."

"Then we get the miners together, and go wipe them out."

"That's about it," Foxx agreed. "And the sooner we move, the better. The miners won't stick together very long. I'd hate to set up a raid on that syndicate hideout and find out just before we started for it that you and me was the only ones going."

"Who's going to keep an eye on Maxine while we're out after the syndicate's gang?"

"That's something I've been trying to figure out. If

bad comes to worse, I guess she could go along with us."

"Damn it, Foxx, we're not going out on a Sunday school picnic!"

"She can stay out of the way, Griff. I'd feel a hell of a lot better if she was someplace close by than if she was back here at the hotel by herself."

"I've got an idea, but you might not like it."

"I won't know until I hear what it is."

"Let the old Shoshone stay here and guard Maxine."

"Damned if I don't think you've got the answer!" Foxx said. "There's only one thing bothers me, though. Pah-na-sha's been counting on getting into that fight, you know. He's not going to like the idea much."

"He listens to you pretty well, Foxx. You ought to be able to persuade him."

"Maybe. When you come right down to brass tacks, though, I haven't got any strings on him. All I can do is try, but I ain't about to mention what we've got in mind for him to do until after he's showed us where the syndicate gang's holed up."

"What do we do while we're waiting for him?"

"We won't be wasting any time, Griff. I'll go out and talk to the two Joes after a while, and you stick around and keep your eyes peeled in case Jed Morgan makes another try."

Pah-na-sha had not shown up when Foxx left for the Two Joes Mine, but Foxx was not impatient. He rode out to the mine, his thoughts running ahead to the impending confrontation with the syndicate gunmen. It was not a fight he was looking forward to. He'd been depending more heavily than he'd allow himself to admit on the territorial authorities' taking a hand in settling the matter.

Big Joe and Little Joe were hard at work. As Little

Joe explained, "Generally, we hire three men to do the coolie jobs down in the shaft. Me and Big, we've done more'n our share of that kinda work. We didn't expect we'd have to go back to it."

"Not that we can't," Big Joe said hastily. "But it ain't right that we got to, all the same."

"Well, if you and your friends can run off them syndicate gunhands, maybe you won't have to go back to it again," Foxx reminded them. "Griff tells me you boys have been busy. How does it look?"

"Looks like we're going to have 'em outnumbered, by God!" Big Joe told Foxx cheerfully. "Foster and Means was hanging back till I told 'em that coulee where the syndicate guns is camping is right between their workings. And Dave Kincaid rode over yesterday and said he'd changed his mind, he's going with us. He'll make up for some of them yellowbellies that backed out."

Foxx had no idea who Kincaid was, but said, "That's real good, Big Joe. How many men does that give us now?"

"Seven, counting you and Griff." Then a note of anxiety crept into his voice as he asked, "That'll be enough, won't it?"

"It oughta be," Foxx replied. "I guess they've all got pretty good guns and plenty of ammunition?"

"Sure. But we've got something better'n guns and bullets, Foxx," Little Joe broke in. "Look here!"

Opening the door of a cabinet that took up most of one wall of the little mine office, the small man took out a rag-swathed bundle. Unwrapping it, he showed Foxx a dozen half-sticks of dynamite fitted with very short fuses.

"Every one of our fellows is going to bring a bunch of these. Them's fifteen-second fuses, Foxx. All of us will light up cigars and we'll start out by tossing these into that bunch of bastards. We ought not have to do much shooting after they go off."

"You just might have what it'll take to win this fight right there in your hand, Little Joe," Foxx told him. "Hell, with a few of these we might not even have to fire a shot!"

"That's what we figured," Big Joe said.

"How soon can your bunch be ready to move?"

"Well, we didn't know how long you was going to be away, so we didn't settle on a day," Little Joe said. "But it'll be good if we can go real soon, before anybody else gets cold feet."

"How does day after tomorrow sound to you?" Foxx asked.

"Sounds real good," Big Joe nodded.

"Can't be too soon for us," his partner seconded.

"Let's say it's settled, then," Foxx told them. "Day after tomorrow. We'll meet here, say about four o'clock, and try to get out to where they're camped just before dark, maybe while they're having supper. Will you men spread the word?"

"We sure as hell will!" Big Joe assured him. "And by the time we get through with them sonsabitches, maybe the syndicate bosses will think twice before they start anything around here again!"

When he started back to Goldsburgh, Foxx gave the livery horse its head, letting the animal set its own pace as he covered the narrow path leading to the main trail. He devoted himself to the problem of the miners, telling himself that once it had been settled, he and Griff would have no more interruptions in their efforts to bring in Jed Morgan.

He reached the turnoff into the main trail, and was kneeing the animal off the side trail from the mine when the horse shied. Foxx grabbed the reins, and had just gathered them into his left hand when as if by magic the old Shoshone appeared on the path in front of him.

"Pah-na-sha!" Foxx exclaimed. "Where in hell did you come from?"

"Wait for you here," Pah-na-sha replied calmly.

"How'd you know I'd be coming this way?"

"Hear you back from where you go, know you be coming this way pretty soon, today, tomorrow maybe."

"Wouldn't it've been easier for you to come see me at the hotel?"

"Shoshone people better off they stay out of white town."

"You might be right at that, Pah-na-sha."

"Now you back, Foxx, we go kill enemies?"

"Pretty soon." Foxx hesitated for a moment, decided that it was not yet time to tell Pah-na-sha exactly what he was planning.

"You bring gun you promise?" the Shoshone asked.

"Yes. It's at the hotel. I didn't know I was going to run into you out here, or I'd've brought it along."

"You give me later. Not need now."

"I'll give it to you later on today, Pah-na-sha. Soon as I get back to town and get through talking to Griff, I want you to show me where the fellows you tracked is camping."

"You want to go now?"

Foxx made another quick decision. He hadn't planned to delay his return, and had intended to take Presser with him when he went with Pah-na-sha to scout the syndicate gunmen's hideout, but as he considered Pah-na-sha's suggestion, he saw no reason why he shouldn't handle the job alone.

"We might just as well go now, Pah-na-sha, seeing we're so close," he said. "But when we get there, I want you to remember that this trip's not for fighting. That'll come later on, after I see what kind of place it is where they've got their camp. You keep that in mind, now."

Pah-na-sha nodded. "I know. Next time, we kill them."

Instead of lying, Foxx said, "You better hop up behind me, Pah-na-sha." The Shoshone vaulted up to the rump of Foxx's horse with a springiness a much younger man would have envied. "All right," Foxx told him. "Just point out which way to go."

Following Pah-na-sha's directions, they rode east for a half hour, then veered south. Foxx tried to determine what landmarks the Shoshone was following, but could not. He gave up the effort, and selected his own against the time when he'd be returning without a guide.

Almost abruptly, within the space of a quarter of a mile, the cedars and juniper bushes that bordered the river thinned out, then disappeared completely. The terrain grew rougher, and huge stone formations loomed out of the barren ocher earth. Meandering crevices widened into canyons or shelved down to broad open coulees. As the livery horse ambled on across the hard soil, Foxx felt naked and exposed by the lack of cover. He was relieved when Pah-na-sha told him it was time to rein in.

"Put horse in canyon," the old Shoshone said. "Better we walk rest of way."

Foxx guided the horse into the first canyon he saw that was wide enough and deep enough to hide the animal, and tethered it to a projecting boulder. He slid the Winchester from its saddle scabbard and tucked it in the crook of his elbow.

"All right, Pah-na-sha," he said. "You go on, I'll follow."

Again Pah-na-sha followed landmarks that Foxx could not identify, and again Foxx chose his own: an odd-shaped boulder, a rock formation, the zigzag pattern of a canyon's rim, a hump on the edge of a coulee. For the next quarter hour Pah-na-sha set a fast pace, leading Foxx in a course that missed being a straight line only when it was necessary to veer around a canyon or other natural obstacle. The Shoshone made no effort to crouch or to hide, but walked erect in long, ground-covering strides.

"Hadn't we ought to be a mite careful?" Foxx finally asked.

"No need. Enemies camped in coulee. Can't see us yet."

"Haven't they got a lookout posted?"

"They careless. Think nobody know where they camp."

"How close can we get to the coulee, Pah-na-sha?"

"We get close. Place on rim we look down, see them good."

A few hundred yards farther Pah-na-sha halted and put a finger across his lips. Foxx nodded. Pah-na-sha began moving ahead, more cautiously this time. Foxx kept a pace or two behind his guide, and when Pah-na-sha crouched and slowed down to a more deliberate pace, Foxx followed suit. They advanced a dozen yards or so, and the Shoshone pointed ahead. Foxx looked and saw the coulee a score of yards distant.

Now Pah-na-sha dropped on all fours. Foxx did likewise. They crawled for only a short distance on hands and knees before Pah-na-sha flattened himself out and began inching forward in a snakelike wriggling motion. Foxx stopped when the Indian did.

"Keep head low," Pah-na-sha said, his voice a soft whisper.

Foxx nodded. He followed Pah-na-sha as the old man crept up to the edge of the drop-off. Below, the wide shallow coulee lay open to their gaze. It was shaped like a bowl, roughly circular, with steeply sloping sides that made the depression invisible from the surrounding ground. The bottom of the coulee was perhaps twenty feet lower than the surface of the soil around it, and forty or fifty yards in diameter.

Along one side a dozen horses were tethered to a picket rope. Foxx saw why the picket line's location had been chosen; just beyond it a spring trickling from the sloping wall had been channeled into a narrow ditch that carried water to the tethered horses. Two tents, facing each other, stood a dozen feet apart in the center of the coulee. Between the tents a fire pit had been dug, but the pit now held nothing but black dead coals.

A tarpaulin had been spread between the corners of the tents and covered most of the space at one side of the fire pit. Four men lounged on the canvas, two more were hunkered down on the bare ground across the fire pit from the tarp, and the legs of a sleeping man stuck out between the flaps of one of the tents. Foxx turned to ask Pah-na-sha why he had told Foxx there were eight men in the gang, but the Shoshone shook his head and laid a forefinger across his lips. Foxx nodded and kept silent. A moment later he understood the reason for Pah-na-sha's signal.

"When in hell's Blanton coming back with the grub he went after?" one of the men on the tarpaulin asked. "My belly thinks my throat's been cut."

Foxx jumped with surprise; the speaker's voice was reaching his ears as clearly as though the outlaw had been standing directly in front of him. He wondered if the desert silence was the reason for the clarity of the transmission, or whether some freak formation of the coulee's sides turned it into a megaphone.

"I heard that new fellow tell Blanton he had a little job to do in town," one of the other men said. "I guess it's taking him longer'n he figured on."

"They sure oughta be back by now," a third put in. "They've had time enough to go clear to Boise City and back."

At the moment, Foxx became less interested in the clarity with which he could hear what was being said than the fact that instead of eight gunmen, they'd now have to face nine. He looked questioningly at Pah-na-sha, who extended his left hand with its palm turned upward and dragged his right forefinger from the crotch of his thumb to the edge of his palm. Recalling the sign language that all Indians understood, Foxx dredged up the meaning of the gesture.

Pah-na-sha was saying, "We'll talk later."

Foxx replied by slashing his stiffened hand downward, the sign for "All right."

Their exchange of signs had taken only a few seconds. Foxx had already turned his attention back to the gunmen before the one who'd spoken first said, "How much longer are we going to be holed up here, anyways? When I taken on this job, it wasn't supposed to last only a week. It's been damn near a month now, and it don't seem no closer to being finished."

"What in hell're you bellyaching about?" one of his companions asked. "You're drawing pay for every day we're here."

"That's right," still another chimed in. "I'd sooner get paid for waiting than fighting."

"It ain't going to be that much of a fight," the second man growled. "Bunch of dirt-grubbers. We'll spook 'em so bad they'll shit their britches running away!"

"Just the same, I want to get it over with," the first man who'd spoken replied. "I got money in my pocket, and money means whiskey and women."

"Ah, you'll feel better after Blanton and Morgan get back with the grub," another said.

"Morgan? That'd be the new man's name, I guess," the first man said. "I don't recall hearing Blanton mention it, at least. Is this Morgan any good? I never heard of him."

"I have," volunteered one of the men, who until now had been silent. "He's all right, he's one of us. Just got out of the pen, back in Nebraska. He'll hold up his end in a fight."

Foxx did not wait to hear anything more. He turned to his companion and brought his hand up to his breast, palm flat and turned to the ground, then moved it back and forth urgently.

Pah-na-sha nodded, and started wriggling back from the edge of the coulee. Foxx wasted no time in joining him. They got to their feet as soon as it was safe to stand, and Foxx began trotting toward the canyon where they'd left the horse.

Pah-na-sha was keeping abreast of Foxx. He asked as they ran, "What he say you get *me-ta-te-dah?*"

"Something I didn't like to hear," Foxx replied. "It's too long a story to tell you now. Come on. I got to get back to town in a hurry!"

By using the landmarks he'd noted when following Pah-na-sha to the coulee, Foxx found his way back to the trail. On reaching it, he reined in.

"I'll ask you to do something for me," he told the Shoshone. "Go tell the two Joes to get their men together tomorrow instead of the day after. Tell 'em I'll send Griff down to explain why, and tell 'em what to do. You got all that?"

"Yes. What I do then, Foxx?"

"Go back to the coulee and keep watch. If them gunmen start anyplace, follow 'em, and then come find me."

"Where I find?"

"Damn it, I don't know! I'll be here or at the hotel, as far as I know. Ask somebody, if you don't run across me."

"No worry, Foxx. I find you."

"Sure. Now go tell the Joes what I told you, and then get back to that coulee."

Foxx showed no mercy to the livery horse on his way back to Goldsburgh. He kept the animal at a gallop where the trail was straight enough, and used a hard hand on the reins to keep the animal on the beaten track where the trail wound like a serpent.

In spite of his fast pace the trip took what seemed to Foxx an interminable time. His horse was flecked with lather and panting hard when it reached the last stretch of straight and fairly smooth road and he could see the town a half mile ahead. Foxx drummed his bootheels against his horse's ribs, trying to urge it to greater speed, but the animal had nothing more to give.

When at last he galloped into Goldsburgh's main street, Foxx saw at a glance that he was too late. A crowd of men was milling around in front of the hotel. Across the street there was a small group of women standing under the awning of the general store, their heads bobbing in spirited conversation. Foxx hauled back on the reins, the tired horse skidded to a halt and stood panting with its head drooping low. Foxx slid out of the saddle.

"What's happened?" he asked one of the men at the edge of the crowd.

"Somebody got shot."

"Who?"

"Damned if I know, mister. I just got here myself."

Foxx pushed through the crowd, using his elbows to clear a path. The slender desk clerk was standing in the lobby, talking to three men. He saw Foxx.

"I'm glad you finally got here, Mr. Foxx," he said. "A terrible thing's happened. We tried—"

"Never mind what you tried. Who was it got shot?"

"Your friend. Mr. Presser."

"How bad was he hurt?"

"I don't know, Mr. Foxx. We took him over to Dr. Jackson's office right away. I haven't heard anything about how he's doing."

Foxx half turned before he remembered to ask, "What about Miss Bowden?" He saw a blank look sweep over the clerk's face and remembered how Maxine had been registered. "I mean, Mrs. Martin, of course."

"I—" The clerk frowned and his face puckered unhappily. "I can't tell you that. Nobody's seen her since the shooting."

"Ain't the doctor's office in that building catty-corner across the street?" Foxx asked the clerk. He barely waited for the man to nod before he was out of the hotel and pushing his way back through the crowd.

Dr. Jackson was a tall, well-fleshed man with a rubicund face topped by a fringe of snowy hair. He came to the door of his inner office in response to Foxx's urgent knocking, a frown on his face.

"Whatever's wrong with you, you'll have to wait. I'm tending to a wounded man back here," he told Foxx impatiently.

"I know that, Doctor. His name's Griff Presser, and I'm his boss. My name's Foxx, chief of the California & Kansas Railroad's detective force. Now, how is he?"

"Not in good condition at all, Mr. Foxx. If you'd like to come back to my surgery—"

Foxx followed the doctor into the narrow rectangular room at the rear of the office. An operating table took up most of its floor. Griff Presser lay on the table, his face ashen, his eyes closed. He was breathing irregularly in labored, whistling gasps. His coat and shirt had been removed and the waistband of his trousers opened.

Bandages were wound tightly around his chest, and Foxx saw the crimson stains where blood from the bullet wounds seeped through the bandages. One of the stains was just left of the center of Griff's chest and the other lower, over his stomach.

"I've been afraid to probe for the bullets," Dr. Jackson said. "The upper wound—well, there's a chance that the bullet missed his heart, but it may have clipped an artery."

"How soon will you know something?" Foxx asked.

"If I told you anything at all, Mr. Foxx, I'd be guessing. All I can do right now is stop him from bleeding badly. If he—"

Griff stirred and the doctor stopped in the middle of his sentence. He went to the operating table and bent over the prone form to listen to Griff's breathing. In the silence of the small room the breaths rasped, seemed to flutter into silence, and then started again. They sounded stronger. Griff opened his eyes and saw Foxx standing beside him.

"I tried—" His voice was thin and ragged, and getting out even the two words he'd said seemed to exhaust him.

"Sure you did, Griff," Foxx said. "Now, don't try to talk. Everything's all right. You rest and sleep and we'll talk about it later."

Griff's mouth opened and he struggled to say something, but a gush of bright blood flooded from his mouth and choked him off. His eyelids fluttered, then were motionless.

Dr. Jackson bent over and rested his ear for a moment on the bloodstained bandage that covered Griff's chest. He straightened up and looked at Foxx, shaking his head.

"I'm sorry, Mr. Foxx," he said quietly. "There was nothing more I could do. Mr. Presser is dead."

CHAPTER 12

In the harsh school that had molded Foxx, women mourned death while men stoically accepted it and, if the death had been caused by an enemy, avenged it. Foxx looked for a long moment at Griff Presser's waxen face, then turned to the doctor.

"He's got a wife in Elko, Dr. Jackson. I guess there's an undertaker that can fix his body up so I can get it sent back there?" When the doctor nodded, Foxx went on, "I'd look on it as a favor if you'd tell the undertaker what I want done."

"Of course, Mr. Foxx. Whatever I can do to help. I'm sorry I couldn't—"

Foxx nodded absently and went on, "I'd take care of it myself, but I got a job that I got to get on with right now. If you'll send your bill over to the hotel, the C&K will pay it."

Leaving the doctor's office, Foxx crossed the street to the hotel. The crowd had dispersed now, only a small handful of the curious remaining. Foxx noted this absently with the same part of his mind that told him that darkness would fall within the next hour or two.

Ignoring the signals of the clerk as he crossed the tiny lobby, Foxx went upstairs. The doors of both the room he and Presser had occupied and the one in which Maxine had been staying stood ajar.

Foxx went by his own room and entered Maxine's.

He stood in the doorway for a moment while he lit a twisted cigar, and looked around. The room was a shambles. The bed was touseled and untidy, the carpet wrinkled. Maxine's valise lay on its side in the middle of the floor, its contents spilled out. Foxx recognized the nightgown Maxine had worn in Boise City in the small pile of feminine garments. There was one shoe, a blouse, the fold of a petticoat. On the dresser he saw the red wig.

There was no sign of blood in the room, just the mute evidence that Maxine had struggled with whoever had taken her, and Foxx had no doubt at all that her captor had been Jed Morgan. He saw the corner of a piece of paper beneath the heap of red hair and slid it out.

"You ain't so dam smart Foxx," he read. "She aint who I was after but shell do. Ill see she dies slow. Yore turns coming."

Foxx identified the sprawled handwriting at once. He tucked the note in his pocket and went into the room he'd shared with Griff Presser.

There nothing had been disturbed. Foxx's bag stood on the floor at one side of the bed, Griff's on the other. The curtain that hung from a rod placed at an angle in one corner to provide a place to hang clothing had been pulled aside, but the garments he and Griff had hung there seemed untouched. The only thing in the room that did not seem usual was the puddle of coagulated blood that covered the floor at one side of the doorway.

Foxx went to his valise and opened it, and found its contents had not been disturbed. He dug out the two boxes of shells that he always carried in the bag, .38 caliber for the Smith & Wesson American Model, .44s for the Cloverleaf Colt. The boxes were too bulky for his pockets; Foxx opened them and emptied one box into each of the side pockets of his coat.

He did not examine the room closely; he didn't need to. From the conversation he'd overheard at the gunmen's hideout and from what his sharp eyes had told him, Foxx could reconstruct what had happened just as though he'd witnessed it. Still, he could not deny his training. When Foxx went downstairs to the lobby, he stopped at the desk to talk to the clerk.

"Did anybody see what happened upstairs?" he asked.

"Not a soul, Mr. Foxx. The only rooms we've got occupied upstairs right now are the ones you and your friends have. Mr. Presser and Mrs. Martin went up right after they came back from the café. That was quite a while after noon, but they'd eaten later than you folks generally do. They went on upstairs, and nobody that I know of saw or heard them before the shooting."

"Who came in through the lobby after that?"

"Nobody, Mr. Foxx!" The clerk's voice was both emphatic and pleading. "I'll swear to that! Not even any of our downstairs regulars came in or went out! Not anybody!"

Foxx did not doubt the man. The back stairway, with its door opening directly into the upstairs hall, had been used by Jed Morgan before. Even if the clerk had kept it locked after the attempt on Maxine's life with the set gun, a man like Morgan could have picked the lock in a few seconds.

"And you didn't hear anything?"

"No, sir." The clerk shook his head. "Not until the shooting. And then I didn't realize right away where the noise came from. As soon as I did, I ran upstairs, and—" The man's voice trickled off to silence, then he said, "I don't really want to talk about what I saw, Mr. Foxx, or even think about it."

"There's no need for you to, right now. Just remember it, because you'll be telling your story in court when I catch the man that's responsible."

"Yes, sir. Of course."

"I'll be away a while," Foxx said. "I ain't leaving town, just going to be away from the hotel here. Move my things into another room, and keep them two rooms locked up till I get back. I'll pay the rent on all three."

Foxx walked down the corner to the Hardrock Saloon and sat down at the table he and Griff had usually occupied. The barkeep brought him a bottle of Cyrus Noble without being asked.

"Sorry to hear about your friend, Mr. Foxx," the man said.

Foxx nodded absently, reaching for the bottle and pouring himself a drink.

"You got any ideas about who could've killed him?" the barkeep asked.

"I'm working on it. He'll turn up sooner or later."

Foxx's tone did not encourage further conversation. Wiping his hands on his apron, the barkeep left him alone. Foxx lit a fresh stogie and sipped the bourbon while he thought.

There had been another man with Morgan, of course. Foxx did not even need to speculate about his identity; the conversation he'd overheard in the coulee earlier had given the accomplice a name, but not a face. Blanton.

There was no need either to speculate on the way that Morgan had made a connection with the syndicate gunmen. In a town that small, a short time spent in a saloon, drinking sparingly and listening carefully, would have given Morgan a very good picture of the tense situation that had developed between the independent miners and the syndicates.

Long ago Foxx had discovered that criminals seek other criminals in the world outside jails and prisons. In the open spaces of the West there were caves, canyons, and shantytowns near small Western settlements, which served the outlaw the same way rooming houses and hotels served him in cities. Morgan must certainly have heard about most outlaw refuges while he'd been in the pen. A casual question, seemingly innocent, a chance encounter with one of the gunmen who'd come into Goldsburgh for supplies, would have been all that Morgan needed to form an association with the waiting hardcases. They, in turn, would have welcomed a man like Jed Morgan to their band.

Foxx did not underestimate the shrewdness of his foe; Morgan was no longer the loutish half-breed he'd captured and sent to prison years ago. The outlaw had learned a lot from others of his kind in the penitentiary.

Foxx suddenly realized he was ravenous. He finished the drink and tossed the cigar stub into a spittoon, then went to the restaurant down the street for supper. He finished his meal, eating more than he really wanted to while he waited for the restaurant's supper trade to thin out.

When Foxx had asked the waiter for a candle, the man had stared in surprise, but went back to the kitchen and returned with a sizable stub. Foxx had taken a half dozen of the .44 cartridges from his pocket and laid them on the table. Clamping the lead slugs between his teeth, he'd twisted the soft lead from the brass cases and set the cases upright before lighting the candle. Then he'd taken a number of wooden matches from his pocket and laid them beside the shell cases.

A small pool of soft wax had dripped down the side of the candle into the saucer that held it while Foxx was busy with the shells. He broke the matches in half and stuck the heads of the halved matches into the shell cases sticking up above the case rims. Working carefully, he collected a bit of soft wax from the saucer and worked it into the cases around the protruding match-heads.

He was still working on the job when the restaurant door opened and Pah-na-sha sidled in. For a moment the old Shoshone glanced around the restaurant, and Foxx realized that his eyes had not yet adjusted to the light of the interior. He signaled, and Pah-na-sha started for the table where Foxx was sitting. He'd gotten halfway across the room when the waiter intercepted him.

"Out," the waiter snapped. "We don't serve Indians here."

"Let him alone!" Foxx called. "He's working for me!"

For a moment the waiter appeared ready to argue, then he nodded and said, "As long as it's you, Mr. Foxx, I guess it'll be all right, as long as he don't expect us to serve him."

"Bring him a steak and some coffee," Foxx said.

Again the waiter hesitated momentarily, but then he nodded meekly enough and started for the kitchen. Pah-na-sha came to Foxx's table, and Foxx motioned for him to sit down. The Shoshone obeyed.

"Enemies got your woman," he said without preamble.

Foxx was not surprised at the news, only that Pah-na-sha had gotten to him with it so quickly. "I sorta figured that out," he said. "But I'm glad you come to tell me."

"All right to stop watch them. They not go tonight."

"Sure. You done right. What'd the two Joes say when you told 'em what I wanted them to do?"

"They say they try. They not know if can do."

"I guess that's the best we'll get." Foxx sat silently for a moment, his mind busy changing plans.

Pah-na-sha eyed the cartridge cases for a moment before he grunted and said, "You spoil good bullets. Why you play so?"

"It ain't just playing," Foxx replied, but did not explain further. Then he asked the Indian, "You feel like going back out there to the coulee with me?"

Pah-na-sha bobbed his head without hesitation. "We go now. Eat on way."

"No. There's time for you to eat right here. Maxine'll be all right for a while. I'd imagine Morgan and Blanton brought some whiskey back from town with 'em."

"They got plenty bottles," Pah-na-sha said, confirming Foxx's deduction.

Before Foxx could ask any more questions, the waiter brought the steak. He did not place it in front of Pah-na-sha, but set it next to Foxx. Foxx pushed the platter in front of the Shoshone, and motioned for him to eat. Pah-na-sha picked up the steak and began biting into it hungrily.

Foxx pushed his own plate aside and lit a cigar. He continued planning while his companion ate, and said nothing until Pah-na-sha had eaten half the meat and was slowing down. Then he asked, "You any good with a rifle, Pah-na-sha?"

"Not shoot one long time. But don't forget how."

"There's one for you over at the hotel. And the new

pistol I got you in Boise City. We'll pick them up before we leave."

"Good."

Noisily, Pah-na-sha sucked the marrow out of the steak bone, swallowed lustily, and looked questioningly at Foxx, who pointed to the potatoes and beans that remained untouched on the plate.

Pah-na-sha shook his head. "Baby food. Meat for men."

Foxx stood up and scooped the .44-cartridge cases into his hand, then dropped them in his pocket. He said, "We'll go, then. On the way we'll talk about what I figure is the best thing to do."

Riding fresh horses that Foxx had rented from the livery stable and leading a third horse for Maxine's use, Foxx and Pah-na-sha rode back along the trail on the first leg of their return trip to the gunmen's hideout. The night was moonless and silent, and they had talked little since leaving Goldsburgh. It was the Shoshone who broke the silence.

"Good we not hurry, Foxx. Comanche learn you how to wait?"

"They taught me a lot more'n that. I don't suppose I could forget any of it, even if I was to try."

"Comanche, Shoshone, one time one people, old men say when I am boy. Talk same, fight same."

Foxx decided the time had come to tell Pah-na-sha the plan he had been working out. He said, "We ain't been in a hurry because I figure it'll be a while before them hardcases get drunk enough to think about the woman. I'll be right sorry if I'm wrong, but if I am, there would be no way the two of us could handle nine of 'em even if they was all stone-cold sober. We won't have help until tomorrow, and maybe not then."

They rode in silence for a few moments before Foxx continued. "I'm counting on them gunhands being drunk. Some of 'em will be worse'n others, but if half the bunch gets real orrey-eyed, that cuts the odds considerable. We won't have any trouble sneaking up to where we watched from this afternoon, except I want to go a little farther around the coulee this time. Right above where they got the picket line."

"We steal horses?" Pah-na-sha asked, anticipation in his voice. "Shoshone as good horse-stealer as Comanche."

"Listen to the rest. We watch and find out where Maxine is, but we won't make a move until most of them fellows are drunk. When they're drunk enough to be real careless, I snake a lariat down the side of the coulee and you hold it while I shinny down and spook the horses."

"How you spook?"

"That's what I fixed the cartridges for. I drag the match-heads across my boot and toss 'em in front of the picket line. The powder flares up like fireworks, and spooks the horses. Works every time."

Pah-na-sha nodded. "Horses scared from fire."

Foxx continued, "When the horses begin bucking and jumping, I cut the picket line and they bolt. You close your eyes while the flares are going off. The gunhands won't know to, they'll be blinded. I start for wherever Maxine's tied up the minute I cut the horses loose. You cover me while I get her back to the rope, and we use it to get us out of the coulee. You oughta be able to cut down a few of the bastards while I'm getting Maxine. Soon as we hit the top of the coulee, we let off a round or two and run for our horses."

Pah-na-sha said nothing for several minutes after

Foxx had stopped speaking, then he grunted, "Good plan. Will work."

"It'll work if we make it work, Pah-na-sha. And if we don't make it work, it ain't going to be because we didn't try."

"Will work," Pah-na-sha repeated.

After he'd outlined his plan, Foxx had nothing more to say. He and the old Shoshone rode the rest of the way in silence.

They tethered the horses in the canyon where they'd left them during their earlier scouting trip, and started for the coulee, carrying the '66 Winchesters and the lariat. Long before they'd reached their destination, their eyes had become accustomed to the faint starlight. Foxx found that he could see enough of the landmarks he'd memorized on their first visit to be sure he could find the horses if he and Pah-na-sha got separated during their retreat from the hideout.

They had covered less than a third of the walking distance to the hideout when the glow of the gunmen's fire became visible. It served them as a beacon, guiding them to the rim of the coulee in a straight line. Concealed by the darkness, they crouched on the edge of the depression and studied the scene below.

Foxx's eyes went first to Maxine. She was clearly visible by the light of the flames that danced in the fire pit between the two tents. She was lashed to one of the tent poles by ropes around her wrists and ankles. Her long blond hair was disheveled, and her face showed signs of the strain she'd been under. Her blouse had been ripped open at the neck, but not badly, and otherwise her clothing did not seem to have been disturbed. Foxx was sure the gunmen had not yet gotten around to raping her.

Apparently the gang had just finished their supper,

for two iron pans were sitting at one end of the fire pit, piled high with tin plates and utensils. Satisfied that Maxine was all right, Foxx's eyes moved from one to another of the renegades, searching for Jed Morgan. He was surprised when he'd tallied nine men. Apparently the gang felt so secure at their hideout that they had not bothered to post a lookout. They were scattered around the fire pit, four of them on the tarpaulin, two in front of the tent opposite the one where Maxine was tied, the other three across the fire pit from the tarpaulin. Their backs were turned to the spot where Foxx and Pah-na-sha crouched, and Foxx decided that one of this trio must be his foe.

There was no conversation around the outlaws' fire at the moment. Liquor bottles were in good supply, and all of the men were drinking heavily.

A man lounging on the tarpaulin broke the silence. "Well, now that you got the wrong woman, what're you gonna to do with her, Jed?"

"We'll keep her around till all of us has had a crack or two at her, then we'll get rid of her," Morgan replied.

Foxx's guess had been right; the man addressed as Morgan was one of the trio whose backs were to Foxx and Pah-na-sha.

"We better get started on her pretty soon, then," another remarked. "Because once I get on her, I don't aim to hurry just because some of you bastards is waiting to take your turn."

"Now, that ain't fair!" the man next to Morgan protested. "I don't mind taking a wet pussy, but I'm damned if I'll wait for one of you long-winded boogers to get off."

"We'll make it fair and square," one of the men lounging on the blanket said. "Deal a faceup hand of poker, and the man with the high hand gets first crack at her, next high hand follows him, and right on down to low hand."

"That sounds fair enough," one of the others agreed. "Only I'm so damn horny right now, I ain't going to stay on long the first time. What about the second round?"

"Why waste time dealing fresh hands after every go? Just keep right on taking turns till we've all had as much ass as we want."

"Suits me," said the outlaw who'd made the first suggestion. "What happens when we're all finished?"

"Like Jed said," the man who'd suggested the poker game replied. "We can get rid of her, if she's still alive."

Foxx whispered to Pah-na-sha, "Damn it, we can't wait for them bastards to get drunk, like we'd planned to do! We'd better go over to their picket line and get Maxine out of there right now!"

CHAPTER 13

Stepping back from the coulee's rim, Foxx and Pah-na-sha moved silently around the sunken bowl until they reached the spot where the gang's horses were tethered. Foxx uncoiled the lariat. Belly-crawling to the rim again, he let the rope down until its end dangled a foot or two above the ground at the bottom of the steep slope.

"I better leave my rifle with you," he whispered to the Shoshone. "It'd just be in my way when I'm bringing Maxine back, and it'll save you having to reload while you're covering me."

"You don't worry," Pah-na-sha said. "I shoot fast, keep them busy."

Foxx laid down the Winchester and took off his coat. He slid the Cloverleaf Colt out of its pouch and worked it into the top of his boot, then took out the fuses he'd prepared and put them in his shirt pockets. He hitched up his gunbelt, bringing the S&W in its cross-draw holster higher to keep it from getting tangled with the rope as he descended.

"Guess I'm as ready as I'll ever be," he told Pah-na-sha. "All you got to do up here is to keep the rope tight."

Pah-na-sha nodded.

Looping the lariat around his hips, Foxx began backing toward the coulee rim. He looked over his shoulder to see how far his feet were from the drop-off. As he turned back and lowered his foot to take the first step down, he saw a strange shadow that seemed to be moving. Foxx held himself poised for a moment, one foot on the rim, the other in midair. The shadow moved again, and Foxx saw a pair of wickedly glowing green eyes reflecting the gleam of the fire on the coulee's floor, and then the shadow took form, a lithe tawny body loomed behind the eyes.

"Cougar!" Foxx gasped. "Behind you!"

Even before he'd finished his warning, the big cat leaped. Its body hurtled past Pah-na-sha and struck Foxx. He brought up his arms to try to ward the cougar off, but it was already on him, its acrid odor filling his nostrils.

Foxx felt his feet slipping. He lurched forward, trying to regain his balance, but one of his feet was already hanging in midair beyond the rim. Against the animal's weight Foxx could not thrust himself forward far enough to hold his position.

Entangled together, Foxx and the cougar rolled down the sloping wall, each of them trying to fight free. Near the bottom of the coulee Foxx's head struck a protruding boulder. He heard the cougar's snarls echoing in his ears, then he knew nothing more.

Foxx's instincts began to work while his eyelids were still too heavy to open. He stirred and tried to move, but his hands and feet did not respond as they should have. His hands were being held uncomfortably high above his head and his feet felt as though they were weighted by a ton of lead. His entire body was one huge aching cramp. Unaware of anything but his discomfort, his brain still foggy, Foxx flexed his muscles and tried again to pull his arms down so that he could press his hands against his aching head. This effort failed too.

He remained motionless, waiting for memory to come back. In a moment it returned in a sudden rush, and for an instant he saw the cougar's green eyes and the sensation of falling swept over him. He squeezed his eyelids tightly for a few seconds, and when he relaxed and saw reddish flickering lights moving from beyond the lids, he knew where he was and what must have happened to him.

He wondered where Pah-na-sha was, decided the Shoshone was able to look after himself, and began to concentrate on his own predicament.

Foxx understood what was wrong with his muscles, and because his brain was functioning again, he no longer tried to move them. He knew now that his wrists were lashed to one of the tent poles after they'd been pulled above his head, and that the weight of his inert body against his legs was pushing down on his feet, immobilizing them. Uncomfortable as his position was, Foxx kept his eyes closed. He needed time to get his strength back and to think, to plan. As long as the renegades thought he was still unconscious, they were not likely to bother with him.

A harsh voice grated on Foxx's ears as one of the men spoke.

"You know, Blanton, it's damn lucky that cougar jumped the son of a bitch. We didn't know he was within ten miles of us!"

"My fault, Lefty. I ought to've posted a lookout."

Foxx caught the note of authority in the second man's voice even before the first one called him by name. He stored Blanton's voice in his memory.

"Nobody's blaming you," Lefty said. "The bastard

ought not have been where he was, after you and Jed finished the job you done in Goldsburgh."

"Well, when something goes wrong, the boss always gets the blame," Blanton told his man. "We got our bacon saved by a fluke this time, no thanks to me or anybody else."

"Oh, hell, there wasn't no damage," Lefty replied. "The cougar got away, but he give us Foxx for a sorta present."

"You could put it that way, I guess," Blanton agreed. "One good thing, we can go ahead and finish our job for the syndicate without anybody else butting in."

"What about Foxx? Are we just going to get rid of him? He might be worth something to the railroad."

"You mean ransom him?"

"Why not?" Lefty asked. "Money's money, whether it comes from the mining syndicate or the railroad. We could maybe pick up a little bit extra on the side."

"You'd never get Jed Morgan to go along with that idea. You know Jed's been after Foxx ever since he got out of the pen. When I went to town with Jed, I promised him I'd leave Foxx for him to handle."

"If it was up to me, I'd say shoot the bastard right now and get it over with!"

This was a fresh voice, one that Foxx did not recognize.

"Plenty of time, Wright. He's not going anyplace."

"He's held up us finishing our job!"

"Not enough to hurt anything," Blanton said.

"Damn it, Blanton, I didn't look for this job to drag on the way it is, or I wouldn't've joined up with this bunch. I got to be pushing on to Brown's Hole. There's a bunch I said I'd meet there for a job over in Dakota Territory."

"You can go any time you want to. Morgan will fill in."

"No," Wright said. "I told you I'd stick till the job's done, Blanton, and I won't back out now."

"Suit yourself."

Bootsoles moving closer grated on gravel. Foxx's ears told him there were three, possibly four, men approaching. The footsteps stopped, and Blanton spoke again.

"You find anything the direction you went, Jed?"

"Nah. Too damn dark. If Foxx had anybody with him, they sure as hell ain't up there now."

A third man spoke up. "Mighta been different if we'd taken time to saddle our horses, like I wanted to. We sure as hell didn't cover a lot of ground."

"We covered all we needed to, Blackie," Morgan snapped.

This was the first time Foxx had heard Jed Morgan's voice since their encounter six years earlier, and it had a deeper tone, sounded older than he remembered, and much more self-assured.

Morgan went on, "I know for a fact that Foxx didn't have anybody with him on this job but the man I shot and the woman. And we got her tucked away."

"That's what I was telling the boys, here. We don't need to worry anymore, now that Foxx ain't still on the loose."

"He might've got some of them dirt-grubbers to come along," Blackie pointed out. "He was over at that mine we shot up the other day."

Blanton said, "He hasn't had time to talk one of the miners into coming with him."

"I don't think he has either, Blanton," Morgan said. "He was by hisself, all right."

"What I want to know is how the hell he found this

place," Blanton said. "That's one of the things I plan to ask him when he comes to, which ought to be pretty soon."

Foxx heard footsteps moving closer to him, and then Morgan's voice, almost in his ear.

"He's still out, all right. He must've got a hell of a whack when he fell."

"Seems to me it's about time for him to come around," a new voice said. "What you got in mind to do with him when he does, Jed?"

"I ain't quite sure yet, Lefty."

Foxx caught himself in time to keep from opening his eyes. His need to look at Morgan was overpowering. He risked opening his eyelids the merest slit. Because of the way his head was bent forward, his field of vision was limited to the ground. At first he could only make out the fire pit filled with dancing flames, then his eyes snapped into focus and he saw the booted feet of his captors standing around the fire.

Morgan was still speaking. "Whatever I do, you can bet it's going to make the son of a bitch hurt for a long time before I get around to killing him."

"Burning hurts like hell," Lefty suggested.

"I've heard skinning hurts worse," another of the gunmen volunteered.

"Ah, who gives a shit what Morgan does with Foxx?" a third voice broke in. "We was getting ready to get ourselves some ass when this fuss started. Let's get back to it."

"Now, I'll go along with Squint on that," another chimed in. "When're you going to deal that faceup round of poker hands you promised us, Blanton? Jed can do anything he wants to with Foxx after we get through with the woman."

"I don't see why we can't have some fun while Jed makes up his mind," Squint said.

Blanton asked, "Make any difference to you when we start screwing her, Jed?"

"Not a bit. She ain't the one I was after. I wanted Foxx's regular woman," Morgan continued. "You know what I had in mind to do to her?"

Blanton replied curtly, "We ought to. You've told us enough times."

Morgan ignored the gang leader's remark and went on, his voice growing angrier as he spoke. "I was going to carve her up Pawnee-style. Then I was going to put her in Foxx's hotel room and wait so I could see him when he found her. He switched women on me, though! I didn't tumble to it till I seen that red wig up in this one's room when we grabbed her. If she was Foxx's woman, I'd wanta make him watch while all of us fucked her, and I'd be the first one to ram a cock into her."

"Looks like he'll get to watch us putting it to this one," a new voice said.

"Shit! It ain't the same thing," Morgan snorted. "This one don't mean nothing to him, she's just a woman that works for him. He wouldn't give a damn if we made her take on three of us at the same time."

Blanton interrupted Morgan's angry monologue. "You don't seem to be in much of a hurry to do anything with Foxx," he said. "The boys might as well have a crack at the woman, then." He paused and went on, "Costa, you're right by my saddlebags there. Reach in and hand me out that deck of cards from the left-hand bag while somebody spreads out a blanket to deal on. Put it right up close to the fire, so everybody can see the cards."

Foxx did not dare risk turning his head to watch

what was going on outside his limited field of vision. He could tell what was happening by the noises the men made. They were moving around, feet grating on the hard soil as they jostled for positions around the blanket, joking among themselves, bragging about what they planned to do when their turns came with Maxine.

Foxx took advantage of their preoccupation with the preparations for the gamble. Moving a fraction of an inch at a time, he shifted his weight from the bonds around his wrists to his feet. Feeling began to flow back into his arms and legs with the needle-prick tingling of muscles reviving. He missed the familiar weight of the S&W in the cross-draw holster on his left side. Flexing his leg muscles, he felt the slim bulk of the Cloverleaf Colt inside his boot pressing against his calf; apparently none of the outlaws had thought to search him very thoroughly.

He managed to raise his head a bit without attracting attention, then flicked his eyes open for brief intervals that lasted no more than a few seconds each. Most of his covert glances were directed at Maxine, tied to the pole of the other tent. Only a dozen feet separated them, but the distance might as well have been a mile. He could see that Maxine was ignoring their preparations; her head was raised, her chin thrust out, her eyes stared into the darkness beyond the area of the fire pit. He did not try to get her attention. To do so might inspire Morgan to torment her in some fashion, even torture her, as a means of satisfying his hatred of Foxx. His quick stolen looks ended when Blanton spoke.

"All right, let's get on with it here!" the leader said. "All of us know what we're doing, but we better settle the rules right now."

"Hell, every man in this bunch knows how poker

hands run," the man called Blackie objected. "Go on and deal!"

"Soon as I say one more thing," Blanton told him. "I'll deal every man a five-card hand, and that includes me. But there won't be no round-the-corner straights or bobtails. High hand gets first go at the woman, second highest goes next, and on down the line. Everybody got that clear?"

One of the men raised his voice above the murmurs of agreement. "How about busted hands? With nine of us in a five-card deal, there's bound to be some."

"Easy enough," Blanton said quickly. "Whoever holds a busted hand throws it in, and everybody with a busted hand gets one more card. High man follows the low hand from the deal, the low men that got the extra cards go after him."

"That's fair enough," someone called out. "Let's get the deal going!"

Foxx could not see the blanket, only a rear view of the feet and legs of the men standing along the side closest to him. It was not a money game, so there was none of the tense silence that holds sway when winning or losing is a serious matter. Foxx could follow the rise and fall of the players' fortunes by the rapid patter that came after each card dealt, though he could not always identify the speakers.

"Four of clubs? Hit me better next time, Blanton."

"Pretty lady! Give me another one to go with her!"

"First ace, ees lucky!" The accent of the man they called Alvarez was unmistakable.

"Deuces is fine for me, if I get enough of 'em."

"Watch out for Blanton, he give hisself a king!"

"Now, that's something I like! In this kind of deal, two tens is right good."

"Just keep on that way, Blanton, an ace or a four next round to go with my deuce and trey!"

"Shit! That lousy six didn't do nothing for me!"

"What the hell good's an ace without nothing to go with it?"

"Damn it, I wanted another ten to go with my pair!"

"Well, that ace busted hell outa the straight I had going."

"Christ, what a game! Two pairs showing, and everybody else wide open!"

"Look at what Blanton's dealt hisself! Three clubs up!"

By the time the third round of cards had been dealt, Foxx could sense the tension growing around the blanket. There were fewer attempts at humor, and when the players were given their fourth cards, they were silent except for an occasional oath or a brief comment on another player's luck.

"That jack fucked you, Lefty, best you can do now is two pair."

"Two pair'd look good, the way the damn cards are running."

"Geeve me one more deucey, Blanton. Eet make me winner."

"Ah, you're screwed, Alvarez. Morgan or Lefty got a better shot than your deuces."

"Jug's working up a straight if his luck holds."

"How about Blanton? He's got a club flush going."

"None of you's got a look-in. I'm going to fill out my straight, this round."

"All right," Blanton announced. "This one is it."

With only one card left to fill out possible winning hands, the outlaws waited in silence. Foxx could hear the faint snap of each card Blanton turned from the deck, and the comments that followed its exposure were terse.

"Ah, shit! That busts me out!"

"Yeah. Me too."

"There's what I needed!" Foxx recognized the speaker's voice; it was Lefty. "Tens and eights, boys!"

Then Morgan said unemotionally, "Two queens oughta keep me in the running."

"Sheet! *No más de las dos* deuces!"

"Now will you look at that! I told you I was going to fill! A six-high straight, by God!"

"I am bust."

"I sure as hell ain't! King-high straight, boys! That puts me on top if Blanton don't fill his flush."

"Quit stalling, Blanton! Let's see that last card!"

"There it is. Busts me, too."

"Well, ain't that a treat! I get the woman first!"

"Stop blowing, Blackie. She won't even feel that little nubbin you call a pecker."

"Just the same, I don't take second helpings from none of you."

"Shut up! Let Blanton shuffle and deal that one card to all of us that busted out."

Foxx heard the riffle of the deck as Blanton shuffled, then the ribald comments began again.

"Gimme a good card this time, Blanton. I wanta have my go at the dame before her cunt's stretched so big I can't feel it."

"Ah, what a shitty card!" Foxx recognized the voice. The speaker was Wright, the perennial grumbler. "Anything's going to be better than a damn trey!"

"Hey, that ain't bad," Squint said in his high-pitched voice. "One-eyed jacks always was my lucky cards!"

"By damn, I don't go last!" Costa chuckled. "I do better than Wright."

"Blanton done better'n anybody," Lefty pointed out. "Give hisself the king of clubs."

"I needed that one the first round, though," Blanton said.

Foxx was beginning to seethe with anger and frustration now. The time was drawing near when the renegades would be releasing Maxine, and he had a vivid mental picture of the treatment she'd get. He abandoned all caution and, opening his eyes, looked at her across the dozen feet of space that separated them. Maxine saw Foxx move his head and dropped her gaze to meet his eyes.

"Don't worry, Foxx," she said. "They're not going to hurt me all that bad. I can stand it."

In spite of her brave words Foxx heard both fear and loathing in her voice. "Just don't think about it," he told her, and was ashamed that he was forced to offer such weak comfort. Blanton began speaking, and he turned and looked openly at the group gathered around the blanket.

"Here's the lineup, now," Blanton was saying. "Blackie's first, then Jug and Lefty."

"He done real good," Wright said sourly.

"Shut up, Wright," Blanton commanded. "After Morgan, it's Alvarez's turn, and I get the woman when he's done with her. Squint goes after me, Costa's next, and Wright, you're last."

"What about seconds?" Lefty asked.

"Anybody that wants another go can draw cards, I guess," the gang leader said. "That's up to you men. I've done all I said I would."

"Let's get started, then," Blackie said. "I'm ready to take her in the tent and strip her down and get my prong in her!"

"Wait a minute!" Morgan broke in. "We'll fuck her

right here on this blanket. Foxx has got to watch her squirming!"

"Hell, no!" Blackie snorted. "I ain't putting on a show for nobody, Morgan!"

"What's the matter, ashamed because you ain't got much?" Jug asked, laughing.

"I got all I need," Blackie retorted. "But there's some things a man likes to do without nobody watching."

"Hell, Jed, let Blackie do it the way he wants to," Blanton said. "You told us the woman don't mean anything to Foxx."

Some of the gang turned to look at Foxx.

"Damned if he hasn't come to," Blanton commented. "Well, he's all yours now, Jed."

Morgan stopped in front of Foxx, and the two men stared at each other. The hatred in his foe's eyes convinced Foxx that Morgan was poised on the ragged edge of sanity. Foxx returned the glare calmly, and Morgan's face twisted into an even uglier scowl than it normally wore, his uneven lips curling to bare big yellowed teeth, wide-spaced, with eyeteeth that stuck down like the fangs of an animal.

Foxx did not move his eyes, but he was aware that the entire gang was watching him and Morgan in their first face-to-face confrontation.

"Five years!" Morgan snarled. "Five years you taken away from me, Foxx! I don't know yet how I'll get them years outa your dirty skin, but I'm damn sure going to do my best!"

Sensing that any reply he made would only goad Morgan to senseless anger, Foxx remained silent.

"You didn't cost me just five years," Morgan went on. "You put my pore old crippled daddy in the jail that killed him. You're gonna wish you was dead a long time before I'm finished."

"Get it over with, Morgan," Lefty called. "I got to wait for Blackie and Jug to get done fucking the woman before I take my turn, and I'm getting tired of wasting time, listening to you mouth off!"

"That's right," Jug seconded. "I don't give a shit whether we fuck her in the tent or outside, but I'm ready to start."

"Oh, hell!" Morgan snarled. "Do whatever you want! I'll wait till later to start on Foxx."

"Well, go on, Blackie," Blanton said. "You're first. Untie the woman and take her in the tent or put it to her here on the blanket, whichever you want."

Blackie drew his sheath-knife as he started for the tent where Maxine was tied. Maxine stared at him like a bird stares at the sinuous swaying coils of a snake that is holding it hypnotized. Blackie bent down to cut the ropes that bound her feet.

Foxx gritted his teeth in helpless anger, and tried to resign himself to what was going to follow.

Blackie began sawing at the ropes. From the rim of the coulee a rifle barked. Blackie pitched forward on his face and lay still.

CHAPTER 14

While Blackie's body was still slumping to the ground, a second shot split the night. Squint had been standing beside the fire pit, looking along the coulee rim for the source of the rifle fire. He dropped like a poleaxed steer.

Most of the renegades were veterans of many shoot-outs. They were not stampeded or frozen into immobility, nor did they waste ammunition by returning the fire from the coulee rim with their revolvers, which lacked the range to be effective at that distance. Except for Alvarez, who still stood in the open, the gunmen dived for cover behind the tents.

When Alvarez saw Squint drop, he scurried for cover too, and the shot that was intended for him kicked up dust a few yards beyond the fire. Minutes ticked away, but after Alvarez joined his companions in their cover, no more shots were fired.

As time had passed and Pah-na-sha made no move of any sort, Foxx had almost become convinced that something had happened to the Shoshone. Now he gave a silent sigh of relief and waited for his backup man's next move.

Silence settled over the coulee. The night was still except for the occasional crackling of the fire when the flames touched a sap-filled knot in a burning branch.

Blanton's voice broke the hush. "There's not but one man doing that shooting. If we scatter and rush him, he can't shoot fast enough to get all of us."

For a moment none of the gunmen replied, then from behind the other tent Wright called back, "He's damn sure been fast enough to get two of us! I ain't rushing him as long as he can see to aim!"

"Douse the fire, then!" Blanton said. "The water bucket's standing right there!"

"Douse it yourself!" Wright called back. "That bastard up there's just waiting for us to get out where he can see us!"

With the outlaws out of sight, Pah-na-sha had been holding his fire. Now, with the coulee's trick acoustics enabling him to hear what they were saying, he let off two shots. The slugs tore through the canvas of the tent walls behind which the renegades were crouching.

"Damn it, Wright!" Blanton called, "the water bucket's close enough for you to reach it! Douse that damn fire! These tents ain't worth shit for cover, that last slug grazed Lefty!"

Suddenly Jed Morgan dashed from behind the tent to which Foxx was tied, grabbed the bail of the water bucket as he passed it, and upended the bucket over the fire pit. The water sizzled as it hit the fire, and a cloud of white steam quickly covered the fire pit. There was not enough burning wood to enable the flames to survive the wetting. The fire smoked and sputtered, but after a moment or two it was reduced to a few glowing embers and several rising white plumes.

"Now, let's go after the son of a bitch that's sniping at us!" Blanton commanded. "Spread out and get moving!"

Booted feet scraped on baked earth as the gunmen began moving toward the back of the coulee. They moved slowly, picking their way through the black moonless night, until their eyes grew accustomed to the faint illumination provided by the starshine.

Foxx waited until the sounds faded, and called, "Maxine?"

"Foxx?" she replied.

"You all right? They didn't hurt you, did they?"

"No. I'm more scared than hurt. I—well, I was so mad at myself for letting them capture me that I didn't get frightened at first. Then when they hauled me out here and I saw the kind of men they were, I really started to worry."

"I'm sorry you had to go through all this. I wish now that when we didn't take Morgan in San Francisco, I'd've sent you back to Chicago."

"I don't," she said unhesitatingly. "I haven't been hurt so far, and now that you and Griff are here, I feel like I'm already out of trouble."

Foxx hesitated for a moment, then said, "Griff's not here, Maxine. Morgan killed him back there in Goldsburgh."

"Oh, no!" Maxine's lips compressed for a moment, then she swallowed hard and said in a voice that showed only part of the strain Foxx knew she must be feeling, "I'm sorry, Foxx. Somehow I feel like I'm partly to blame."

"You're not, so don't feel like you are. It was me that put Griff on the job. He knew what he was up against."

"I guess you're right, Foxx. I'll try not to think about it, at least not right now."

"Good. Now tell me how Morgan got to you."

"He and that Blanton must have come up the back stairs, because that's how they took me. I'd told Griff I was going to my room and lie down, and I did. He told me not to worry, that he'd leave his door open a crack so he'd see anybody who might be in the hall."

"I wondered about that," Foxx said. "On a job like this, Griff wouldn't open the door if somebody knocked unless he'd had his gun ready. That damn Jed Morgan can move like an Indian. He seen Griff's door was cracked open. He sneaked past your room and shot Griff through the crack."

"Well, I went to sleep," Maxine continued. "I don't know how long I slept, but something woke me with a start. Before I was really awake, Blanton had broken into my room and had his hand over my mouth. Then Morgan came in and said they'd better get moving fast. They carried me out and Morgan threw me across the back of his horse and they took the back way out of town."

"Likely what woke you up was the shot that killed Griff."

Maxine asked, "If that's not Griff shooting from up there, who is it?"

"Pah-na-sha."

"You mean the old Indian?"

"Yes. With Griff dead, he was about the only man I'd've trusted to come along with me on a job like this."

"How did they capture you, Foxx? I thought you were dead when they brought you here. You just lay there without moving, and it wasn't until they lifted you up to tie you to the tent pole that I realized they wouldn't be tying you up if you were dead. What happened to you, Foxx?"

"I was just knocked out. Must've hit my head when I tangled with that cougar."

"What cougar? Where? When?"

"It's too long a story to tell you now, Maxine. There'll be time for that later on."

"I hope so. Foxx, we've got to get away before they come back. That Jed Morgan is crazy. He won't stop until he's killed both of us."

"I've been trying to get my hands free, but my fingers are too numb," Foxx told her.

"Mine are too. I worked at this rope around my wrists until I couldn't feel it any longer, but the knots are still just as tight as they were when Morgan tied me up."

At the back of the coulee a shot sounded, the flat report of a revolver, then there was another, and a few moments later, a third. Foxx heard the gunmen calling to each other, but could not make out what they were saying.

"Damn!" Foxx said, his voice worried. "I hope that don't mean they've spotted Pah-na-sha!"

Another distant revolver-shot echoed from the darkness, and there were more muffled shouts from the renegades.

"It's bad news for us if that bunch catches up with Pah-na-sha," Foxx said. "There's too many of them for him to handle alone."

"Pah-na-sha not there. Am here."

Pah-na-sha's voice was so near that for a moment Foxx was unable to believe what he'd heard. A few seconds later the old Shoshone materialized out of the darkness beside the tent.

"I don't know how you got here, but I'm sure glad to see you," Foxx told him.

"Get here easy. Enemies chase shadows."

"You mean Blanton's bunch is just milling around out there, shooting wild?"

"Maybe shoot bushes. Maybe shoot each other."

Pah-na-sha drew his sheath knife and began cutting the ropes that bound Foxx's wrists to the tent pole. "We go shoot them now."

"Soon as we get Maxine loose. And soon as I can get my hands on one of them Winchesters."

"Long guns up there," Pah-na-sha said, pointing to the back of the coulee. "Too big carry, hide them. You got no gun?"

"All I got now is my little Colt, and it ain't much good for the kind of shooting we'll have to do."

"Look in the tent, Foxx," Maxine said. "I saw Jed Morgan throw your gun in there before they tied you up."

Foxx's wrists were free now, and he began rubbing them to restore feeling to his hands.

"You cut Maxine free," he told Pah-na-sha. "I'll see if I can find my pistol."

Foxx lifted the tent-fly and groped along the floor until he found the gunbelt with his S&W still in its holster. He buckled it on as he walked across to the other tent, where Pah-na-sha had just finished severing the ropes binding Maxine.

"We better move fast," Foxx told his companions. "Blanton and his bunch ain't fired a shot for quite a while, and that means they'll be heading back this way any minute."

"We go out coulee mouth," Pah-na-sha suggested. "Not run into them coming back."

"Good idea," Foxx replied. "If we get up on the rim, we can keep 'em penned up in here till daylight. By sunrise the Joes oughta be here with the miners, and we can finish this fight once and for all."

"We take horses, enemies don't get away," Pah-na-sha said.

"You're dead right, Pah-na-sha!" Foxx agreed.

"Come on! Let's do it! We'll take the nags out of the mouth of the coulee, then circle around the rim and take Blanton and his men from behind!"

They had no time to waste with saddles or bridles. The horses had been tethered to the picket line with rope halters, and before cutting the line Foxx gathered the ties of the three nearest the end and slipped them off the picket rope. He handed the cut end of the picket line to Pah-na-sha.

"Pull that line into a loop," he said. "We'll lead the ones we ain't riding until we're outside the coulee, then we can let 'em run loose."

Leaving a freed horse with Pah-na-sha, Foxx led the other two over to where Maxine stood. "I can't ride a horse, Foxx," Maxine said, her voice sharp with concern.

"I'll put you on his back," he told her. "Just don't let the horse know you're nervous."

"But don't we need saddles, Foxx?"

"There's no time to fool around with saddles. Don't worry. You'll stay on his back all right."

Lifting Maxine to the back of the horse, he looped the halter around its muzzle and handed her the loose end.

"What am I supposed to do?" she asked, bewildered.

"Just clamp your legs on him tight as you can, and hang on," he told her. "We ain't going to be moving fast. If you get in trouble, me or Pah-na-sha will be close enough to give you a hand."

With Pah-na-sha in the rear leading the other horses, Foxx led the way to the narrow mouth of the coulee. They reached it just as shouts went up from the outlaws returning to camp. As they passed through the cleft and turned to circle back along the rim, the angry hubbub intensified.

"I guess that means they found out they lost their horses," Foxx told Maxine. "I'd say we got out just in time."

"Do you really think we can keep them in that valley until somebody gets here to help us?" she asked.

"Sure. Most of 'em anyway. They're smart enough to know they can't get away without horses."

"What do you think they'll do?"

"Sit tight till daybreak. There's not much else they can do. If I was in Blanton's boots, I'd wait till there's enough light to see by and then send two or three men to the closest mine to steal a team and a wagon."

"A wagon? Wouldn't that be awfully slow?"

"It'd be slow, but they'd be able to carry their saddle gear to the nearest place where they could get some horses."

Pah-na-sha called to Foxx, "We come far enough now. We let horses go?"

"I guess this is as good a place as any. I'll hang back and take the halters off of 'em."

Foxx let Pah-na-sha get ahead of them, and as the horses came up, leaned over to pull the loops of the halters over the heads of the horses one at a time. The liberated animals followed along for a short distance, then began to scatter. After the last of the horses had been cut loose, Pah-na-sha dropped the picket rope and they rode abreast for the rest of the way around the coulee.

"Let's get ourselves located now," Foxx said. "Where'd you hide the rifles, Pah-na-sha?"

"Little way in front. Find easy."

"Here's what we better do," Foxx told them. "Pah-na-sha, you go on back to the mouth of the coulee.

Not right in it, but on the highest part of the rim to one side. Me and you, Maxine, we'll go to the back rim."

"Then we start kill them, Foxx?" Pah-na-sha asked.

"Damn it, there's seven of them and three of us!" Foxx told the Shoshone. "That ain't as big odds as it was before you knocked over them two from the rim, but killing's their business, and I'd say that makes the odds a little bit bigger in their favor."

"One bullet kill one man, Foxx."

"Sure. But we ain't got enough ammunition to hold out in a long fight. All we're out to do is keep them men from getting outa that coulee."

"They try, we shoot. Then we kill them."

"If they do try, we don't have much choice. But I don't think they'll do much till it starts getting light. By then the two Joes oughta have the miners here."

They'd been moving slowly around the rim of the coulee while they talked. Now Pah-na-sha reined in.

"You wait. Get long guns."

A yard or so away from where they'd stopped, a rock outcrop shoved up at a sharp angle from the barren soil. The Shoshone dismounted and took the step or two necessary to reach the formation, and from some crevice that only he could see in the dim starlight, produced the two '66 Winchesters.

Foxx said, "You keep one and give me the other one. I'll give Maxine my S&W. This .38 ain't got enough range to do much good, but all they'll see down in the coulee is the muzzle blast."

Foxx went on, speaking more to Pah-na-sha than to Maxine, "I guess we better waste a shell or two apiece when we get in place, just to let them fellows know we're up here. You shoot at the first man you see move, and then I'll wait a minute and let off a round, and Maxine can follow me. After that, we won't shoot until they give us a reason to."

They split up then, Pah-na-sha returning to the mouth of the coulee while Maxine and Foxx continued around the rim. They reached the spot, roughly half-way from the mouth, where Foxx intended to leave Maxine, and he reined in.

"You sure you'll be all right, staying here by yourself?" he asked her.

"Of course I will! I'm not afraid of the dark, and I don't scare easily." Maxine paused thoughtfully, then went on, "I had a nasty feeling when they first started talking about taking turns raping me. Then they brought you in, and I guess I was too worried about you to be scared. After that things happened so fast that I don't remember feeling much of anything."

"You didn't act scared, I'll give you that."

"Well, I'd have tried not to show it, if I had been. But you don't need to worry about leaving me here. I'll be able to do what I'm supposed to."

"Just one thing, Maxine," Foxx said soberly. "Keep a real careful lookout, and keep listening, too. If you see one of them coming toward you, shoot him. If you hear anything that sounds like somebody sneaking up, let off a shot and I'll get to you as fast as I can move."

"I will."

He kissed her gently. "Now I got to get on around to where I'm supposed to be. Just remember what I told you to do, and you'll be all right."

Foxx rode over to the station he'd chosen for himself, and tethered the horse. He walked up to the rim of the coulee and gazed into blackness. Though he was able to see reasonably well within a radius of five or six yards along the rim, the starshine was not bright enough for him to see the coulee's floor. He thought he could make out the tents as vague, formless patches, a bit lighter in hue than the earth on which they stood, but was not really certain that he was seeing them or just remembering where they were located.

He was still trying to pierce the darkness when Pahna-sha's rifle cracked. Foxx did not know whether the Shoshone had seen movement in the coulee or had simply grown tired of waiting, but he waited a moment before aiming at the spot where he thought he could see the tents and fired the round he was supposed to.

Fixing his eyes on Maxine's position, Foxx waited for her to fire. Seconds passed and there was no shot. Then he heard the bark of the S&W and saw the red spurt of muzzle blast, and relaxed. Raising the Winchester's muzzle, his eyes darted back to the coulee's floor, but as had been the case when he and Pah-na-sha fired, the shot was ignored by the syndicate's hired gunmen.

The false dawn showed its illusory promise, and through the brief period of gloom that followed until the true dawn brightened the sky, Foxx paced the canyon rim. He kept scanning the floor of the coulee, but it was still veiled in shadows. Tightening his jaw, he hefted the rifle in the crook of his elbow and kept pacing.

Slowly the sky lightened and the shadows on the floor of the coulee brightened to make details visible. Foxx saw no sign of men or movement. The area around the tents was deserted. The bodies of Blackie and Squint had been removed. Then as his eyes reached the coulee's mouth, Foxx stopped and stared. During the few hours of darkness during which they'd had to work, the gunmen had been busy. Dropping to one knee, Foxx examined what the renegades had done.

Blanton's men had erected a breastwork, a crescent of small boulders, near the mouth of the coulee. The stones were not piled high, but the wall rose high enough to shelter men lying prone behind it. The breastwork's location was well chosen, for the rim slanted sharply downward at the mouth. Within easy rifle range of the low stone crescent there was no place where an attacker could fire from above at the men behind it without exposing himself to their shots.

Even though he'd been expecting them, the first shots from the breastwork took Foxx by surprise. A bullet pocked the rim inches from his feet, and another whistled past his head. Foxx dropped flat, and as he began to crawl up to peer over the rim he heard Pahna-sha's rifle bark and its slug's shrill ricochet as it glanced off the breastwork.

Another bullet from the coulee's floor plowed into the dirt near Foxx's head, and he stopped his advance and hugged the ground while he backtracked. He had not realized that his position was so exposed. He lay still for a moment before raising his head to look across the coulee, trying to locate Maxine and Pah-na-sha, but could see neither of them.

"Damned if this ain't a Mexican standoff!" Foxx muttered after he'd thought the situation through. "They can't get to us as long as we stay where we are and keep low, but we can't get a shot at them unless we stand up high enough for them to see us and shoot back. They can't come out of the coulee without us picking them off, and we can't go in after 'em as long as they stay back of that wall they've built!"

A shot from Pah-na-sha's position followed by two shots from the renegades broke Foxx's thoughts. He rose to a crouch, but quickly dropped flat again when a slug from the breastwork sent up a spurt of dirt beside him.

Worried about Pah-na-sha and Maxine, Foxx craw-fished back a bit farther from the rim and stood up. He could not see either of them. He waved his hat to attract their attention, and saw Pah-na-sha rise and return his signal with an upraised arm. He looked again at the place where Maxine should be, and breathed easier when he saw that she was standing now, well back from the coulee rim, waving at him.

Hoping they would understand his signs, Foxx raised his arms to his chest and with his palms flattened away from himself, pushed out from his chest. Pah-na-sha got the message at once and began moving back from the rim. Foxx waited until Maxine was looking directly at him and pointed to the Shoshone before he repeated his signal. Maxine nodded and began retreating from the coulee's edge.

Before starting for the horse he'd tethered well back from the edge of the coulee, Foxx retrieved his coat. It was where he'd laid it before his ill-starred descent into the coulee. He slid his arms into the sleeves, and while walking to the horse, dug out a stogie and lit it.

Foxx was still riding around the edge of the coulee when he heard the thuds of hoofbeats. He waited, and in a few minutes the two Joes were reining in beside him.

"Sorry we didn't do better," Big Joe apologized. "We was gonna wait for some more to show up, but I figgered we better get here in case you needed some help."

"We heard some shooting a little while back," Little Joe said. "I guess we done right, didn't we, Foxx?"

"You did. The damned renegades forted in during

the night, and it's going to take a little doing to get at 'em."

"What kind of fort?" Big Joe asked.

"Boulders and shale."

"Hell, we move that kind of loose rock every day of the week." Little Joe reached into his saddlebag and produced one of the small bombs he'd shown Foxx the day before. "One or two of these oughta do the job."

"They just might, at that. Let's figure out how we can get 'em to where they'll do the most good."

A half hour of planning produced a scheme. Leaving the Joes and Maxine at the mouth of the coulee across from the renegades' improvised breastwork, Foxx and Pah-na-sha circled the rim to a position above the gunmen. Foxx took out two stogies and lit them. He handed one to Pah-na-sha.

"Now, don't hold on to that damned bomb too long," he warned the Shoshone. "Little Joe says that fuse won't burn past a count of ten. I hope you know how to count that high."

"Know numbers, Foxx," Pah-na-sha said with great dignity. He counted from one to ten. "You see?"

"I see. All right. I figure it'll take us a count of six from where we start to get to where we throw these things. I'll go first, and you count three before you start. You got that?"

"Yes. But why you go first, Foxx? You forget how to ride like The People. Better me go first."

Foxx decided quickly that he owed Pah-na-sha that much. He nodded. "All right. You go first."

They walked their horses up to the edge until Foxx could see Maxine. She was standing where he'd placed her, well back from the rim of the coulee and upslope from the mouth, where she would be out of the renegades' field of fire. Foxx waved and Maxine raised an arm in reply. In a moment Little Joe and Big Joe began firing at the breastwork from their positions just below Maxine. The renegades began shooting back.

Foxx called to Pah-na-sha, "Go on and ride!"

From the moment he heard the hoofbeats of Pah-na-sha's mount start down the slope, Foxx counted three. He touched the fuse of the dynamite bomb to the glowing tip of his twisted stogie and kicked his horse in the flanks.

Many years had passed since Foxx had ridden Comanche-style, without a saddle, a hand locked into the animal's mane, his body stretched straight forward, one leg hooked over the back of the horse holding him on. He fought to hold himself in place as the horse galloped down the slope, gaining speed with each stride.

Clinging precariously to the horse's back with one hand, the bomb sputtering in the other, Foxx counted to six and tossed the bomb in the general direction of the breastwork.

He'd barely gotten rid of the short-fused sticks of dynamite when the bomb thrown by Pah-na-sha exploded. The concussion set his horse to rearing, and Foxx was almost thrown. The bomb he'd thrown went off with a rolling boom, and the already panicked horse reared more violently. Foxx dug his heels in and struggled to keep the beast under control.

Pah-na-sha had reined in a short distance ahead. He was holding the Colt Foxx had given him, and Foxx drew his S&W as he approached the Shoshone. Pah-na-sha kicked his horse as Foxx came up, and the two swept in a short curve into the mouth of the coulee. Big Joe and Little Joe waved their rifles as they came galloping across the opening to join them. Four abreast, they entered the coulee.

Around the tumbled stones of the demolished

breastwork four of the gunmen were staggering, dazed. Foxx recognized them as Wright, Costa, Jug, and Alvarez. Two others lay on the ground. Foxx left the men who were still on their feet for his companions to deal with, and rode up to the breastwork. The bodies were those of Blanton and Lefty. Morgan had disappeared.

CHAPTER 15

Foxx was not yet ready to give up on Morgan. He stared at the bodies for a moment, lifted his eyes, and stood studying the floor of the coulee while he drew his Smith & Wesson. He ejected the cases of the cartridges Maxine had fired and replaced them with fresh shells.

"You men can handle these four," he called to the Joes and Pah-na-sha. "Not much use to tie 'em up yet. They can dig graves for the two that was killed. And I got a hunch there's two more in them tents that'll have to be buried. I'll go over and look, and see if there's a shovel they can use."

There was only one place on the floor of the bare coulee where Jed Morgan could be hiding. Foxx kept his eyes fixed on the tents as he approached them, watching for a telltale billow of their canvas walls that would betray the movement of someone inside them. The canvas walls hung totally still, but Foxx drew the S&W as he got closer to the tents and kept his finger on the trigger while he drew aside the flaps of one, then of the other.

Morgan was not in either tent. In one the blanket-shrouded bodies of Blackie and Squint lay in the center of the earth floor, surrounded by a scattering of personal gear belonging to the renegades: two rifles, a pistol belt, a pair of almost-new boots. There were several sets of saddlebags; dirty shirts and long johns trailed from some of them.

In the other tent Foxx found a dozen or more empty whiskey bottles, a half-full keg of water, a partly used sack of flour, a bag of cornmeal, another of beans. A few potatoes lay on the ground, as did some airtights containing peaches and tomatoes, the scrag end of a hambone, and the rind left from a side of bacon. There was also an ax and two shovels.

Foxx picked up the shovels and walked slowly back to what remained of the bombed-out breastwork. Little Joe was holding a rifle on the four surviving gunmen, who sat in a row a short distance from the scattered stones where Big Joe and Pah-na-sha were pulling Blanton's body free from the boulder that had crushed out his life. Maxine stood a small distance from both groups, holding the reins of the horses.

Foxx let the shovels fall to the ground and told Little Joe, "Like I thought, there's two more bodies in one of the tents."

"Two more graves, I guess," the miner said. "Or we can just dig two real deep ones and put two bodies in on top of each other."

"Handle it any way you want," Foxx told him. He looked at the torn-up earth where the breastwork had stood. "The ground's already softened up here, I guess it's the easiest place to dig. And if you're going to stack two bodies up in one grave, you might as well have them dig a little more and toss all them busted guns in too."

"I don't imagine the folks we're planting in the ground will care," Little Joe remarked. "What bothers me is how we're going to handle the ones we've caught."

"They'll have to go to jail. What'd you think was going to happen to 'em?"

"Have you seen that Goldsburgh jailhouse, Foxx?"

"No. The constable's been sick, and went up to Boise City for some special doctoring. He's the only lawman in Goldsburgh, so I haven't had much reason to go look at the lockup."

"It's not much of a lockup. Now, if you want these bastards kept safe, we've got an old powder magazine at the mine that me and Big Joe put up when there was a lot of powder being stole. It's made out of boiler sheet and railroad ties, and it'll hold a herd of wild steers. We'll hold 'em there till the marshal can come take 'em to Boise City, if you say the word."

"Whatever word you need from me, you got it. And thanks."

"None needed," Little Joe said. "I don't want these damned gunhands bothering us again, that's why I offered. Right now, I guess I'll get 'em started digging."

"If you want somebody to go with you—" Foxx began.

"Don't worry, they won't give me any trouble," Little Joe replied. "They know how easy it'd be to dig a few more graves."

After the little miner had started the prisoners digging, Foxx walked over to where Maxine stood.

"There's a little job of work I've been saving for you and me to do," he said. "Me and Pah-na-sha left our horses quite a ways from the coulee when we come here yesterday. I thought we could take the Joes' horses, go get ours, and save us a lot of trouble later."

"You're just trying to get me out of the way while the dead men are being buried, aren't you, Foxx?"

"Since you figured it out, I'll own up. But we ain't

had a lot of time to talk. I thought it'd be a good idea."

"It is. There are a few questions I've been wanting to ask you. Besides, I think it'd do me good to get away from this place for a little while."

"I imagine you're right. Let's mount up and go."

"What happened to Jed Morgan?" she asked Foxx as soon as the horses left the coulee. "He's not here, and neither is his body."

"Looks like he slipped away."

"But when, Foxx? Surely the other men wouldn't let him just walk off, when they knew there was going to be more fighting!"

"My guess is that Morgan made up some kind of excuse to go off by hisself. Like he wanted to do a one-man sneak and grab you again, so they'd have a hostage. Or maybe he said he'd go out and try to find a way for them to get past us."

"Wouldn't the others suspect he might be deserting them?"

"Jed Morgan's a good liar, Maxine. He wouldn't have too much trouble framing up a yarn that'd sound good. Blanton was the only smart one in the bunch. If Morgan could make up a yarn good enough to fool him, it'd take in all of the others."

"Have you asked the ones who're left?"

"Not yet. I'm putting that off until they finish burying the dead ones. I want to get them to answering questions while they're tired and put out. Burying's not a nice job, you know, and somebody that's just put four friends in the dirt is going to be more'n a little bit on edge. That makes for honest answers."

"But, if Morgan's loose, Foxx—"

Foxx interrupted. "I know. He'll keep after me.

Well, I don't mind that. I've had men after me before.
The thing that bothers me is that Morgan might be after you this time, too."

"Why? He knows now that I'm not Vida Martin."

"Sure he does. But a man like Morgan don't like to
be made a fool of, Maxine. You getting free from him
just might've riled him so much he'd be bound and determined to get you back."

"Why?" Maxine repeated. "He knows I'm not Vida
Martin, that I'm just somebody you hired to pretend to
be her."

"Which ain't to say I don't think a lot of you, Maxine."

"You don't have to flatter me, Foxx."

"And I ain't. We've gone through a lot together, and
I've got a real special feeling for you. But even if I
didn't have, my guess is Morgan would still come after
you."

Maxine sighed. "I suppose you could be right, Foxx.
You know more about the way Morgan thinks than I
do."

"Anyhow, now's not the time to worry," Foxx told
her. "As soon as we're finished here, you and me will
go back to Goldsburgh. We'll talk about it more then."

They got the three horses Foxx and Pah-na-sha had
hidden in the canyon, and on the slow ride back Foxx
steered the conversation to more pleasant things. They
reached the coulee to find the prisoners just throwing
the last shovelful of dirt on the new graves. Leaving
Maxine to look after the horses again, Foxx began his
questioning. He remembered that Wright had been dis-
satisfied with the way the job of intimidating the independent miners was going, and chose him first.

"You ever do time in the Idaho Territory's pen?"

Foxx asked after he'd taken Wright out of earshot of the others.

"No."

"You've heard what it's like, I suppose?"

"No."

"Well, I never was in it myself, but folks say it's as bad as the Arizona pen down at Yuma City. And I know damn well you heard about it, there ain't anybody on the wrong side of the law that hasn't."

"I've heard."

"Too bad you'll be in the pen here instead of meeting your friends that's waiting for you at Brown's Hole. You and the rest of your bunch likely'll get twenty years," Foxx said calmly, touching a match to a stogie. When Wright did not reply, Foxx went on, "Yep. You'll be an old man when you get out, Wright. And there won't be no pardon, the C&K Railroad will see to that."

"Now, wait a minute! I never did your damn railroad a bit of harm, Foxx!" Wright protested.

"I say you did. You and the others killed a C&K man. You was trying to shut down some mines that pay us a lot of money every year to haul their freight. If that's not enough, I got my own personal reason to see you men do a lot of time."

"It wasn't any of us that was down on you, Foxx. It was that damn Jed Morgan. He fucked up this whole job for us!"

"Where'd Morgan go when he pulled out last night?" Foxx asked suddenly.

"I don't know! Nobody does! We didn't even know he was going to sneak off and leave us holding the bag!"

"You must've heard him say something about what

he was going to do after he got even with me," Foxx suggested.

Wright's brow furrowed as he thought. Then he shook his head. "No. About the only thing Morgan ever talked about was getting you."

"You think back," Foxx told him. "If you think about something he might've let drop that you've forgot right now, let me know. I'd be real inclined to help anybody that'd give me a line on where I might start looking for him."

Although Foxx questioned the other survivors as closely as he had Wright, they gave him much the same story. The only fresh clue he got—if it could be called a clue—had come from Costa.

"Jed was fit to be tied right after you and the woman got away," Costa had said. "He swore he'd keep after you until he got you, and said he didn't give a damn what happened to him afterward."

After the unpleasant work at the coulee had been finished, as they were getting ready to start back to Goldsburgh, Foxx asked Pah-na-sha, "Who's the best tracker in your tribe?"

With neither hesitation nor embarrassment, Pah-na-sha replied succinctly, "Me."

"You sure?"

"Sure. Old Shoshone know tracking. Young men don't learn."

"I got a hunch Morgan's going to hole up a few days. Can you pick up his trail from where he left the coulee and find his hidey-hole for me?"

"Can find."

"Morgan's half Kiowa. He'll know how to cover his sign."

Pah-na-sha spat. "Kiowa children."

"I don't want you to kill him, now. Just find where he's holed up and get word to me. Is there somebody you can take with you to send a message?"

Pah-na-sha nodded. "Grandson."

"You better start now, before Morgan's trail's cold. When you find him, send word to me at the hotel. If you don't find him before two days are up, come back and we'll track him together."

"Understand."

Foxx watched Pah-na-sha as the Shoshone wheeled his horse and started out of the mouth of the coulee. He rode back to where Maxine was waiting with the rest of the party.

"You put the old Indian on Morgan's trail, didn't you?" she asked him.

"Yes. Morgan must've been in a big hurry when he sneaked outa here. I don't imagine he took time to cover his tracks."

"What happens when you catch up with him, Foxx?"

"I'll bring him in to stand trial for Griff's murder."

Maxine looked at him. Foxx saw the question in her eyes, but she left it unasked. They rode silently at the rear of the party through the bright sunlit afternoon until they reached the trail to town. At the branch that led to the mine, the two Joes herded the prisoners onto the fork while Foxx and Maxine continued to Goldsburgh. They'd almost reached the town when she turned to face Foxx.

"Foxx. Now that you've broken up the syndicate's gang, I don't suppose you'll be needing me anymore, will you?"

"It looks like the case is just about closed. The syndicates will lay low for a while after this, I'd imagine.

They'll try to force the independents out again, but they'll find a different way to go about doing it."

"You didn't answer my question."

"I thought I did. The case is finished, and you and me will be heading back home now. We've both got jobs to think about."

"You're not going back until you catch up with Morgan," she said. "I've learned enough about you to know that."

"Morgan's not part of the case, Maxine. He's not the C&K's problem. He's mine."

"And mine, too, after what he did to me. Foxx, I want to help you find him."

"Pah-na-sha's taking care of that."

"Morgan's got a day's start on him. And Morgan's after you. Griff's dead, and you don't have anybody except me to help you."

"What makes you think I need help? I've been handling cases a long time by myself."

"But this one's different. Isn't there something I can do to help you, Foxx? Even if you just use me for bait, the way you started out to do."

"Maybe I made a mistake doing that, too, Maxine. I didn't aim to get you into the kind of fracas this thing turned into. I wouldn't want to do it again."

"Well, I didn't enjoy it, but things turned out all right. I'm volunteering, Foxx. Are you going to turn me down and send me back to Chicago, or let me stay and help you take Morgan?"

Ahead of them Foxx saw the straggling lines of buildings and houses that made up Goldsburgh. He said, "Let's not talk about it any more right now. We've covered so much ground since we had any decent food or any rest that we can't see things real straight."

"I suppose you're right about that. I just realized I'm starving, and after being hauled over half of Idaho, I've got a layer of dirt on me that I'd like to wash off."

"Me too. You want to eat first, or clean up and change clothes first?"

"Let's eat before we go to the hotel. Then we won't have to go out later on."

After their meal Foxx and Maxine sat in his hotel room, relaxing for the first time since her abduction. Maxine wore a flowing negligee of blue satin that brought out the glow in her fair clear skin. She had not done up her long blond hair, which fell in rippling waves down her back. Foxx was in his shirt sleeves, and had not put on his boots. Maxine reached for her drink; Foxx was holding his in his hand. She looked at the compact little Cloverleaf Colt that lay beside the bottle of Cyrus Noble on the table between them.

"I hope you don't think you'll need that tonight," she said.

"So do I. And it ain't likely I will. Morgan's on the run; he'll be too busy saving his own hide to make any trouble."

"Then, let's just forget about everything but ourselves tonight."

Foxx drained his glass and reached his hand across the table to take Maxine's. She set her glass down and came around the table to stand in front of him.

"I never have thanked you for keeping those outlaws from raping me," she said.

"You know you don't need to."

"But I want to."

Bending down, Maxine pressed her lips to his. Her negligee gaped open at the neck, revealing the swell of her full breasts, which Foxx's hands sought and began to caress.

Maxine's fingers were busy with the buttons of Foxx's fly. When she liberated him, he was not fully erect. She pulled her negligee open and leaned over him, swaying so that the tips of her breasts brushed against Foxx's manhood.

"You're not quite hard yet, Foxx, but I don't want to wait, I want you in me now," she said, breathing unevenly.

"I'll be hard by the time I get into you. Go ahead."

Maxine sighed as she lowered her hips to take him into her. She moved slowly and deliberately, prolonging his penetration. Foxx was still swelling as he slipped into her, and continued to grow harder as Maxine's soft buttocks settled on his thighs.

"Oh, this is wonderful!" she whispered, her lips brushing his ear.

For a few moments Maxine did not move. She began to rock her hips slowly, then more quickly as her excitement mounted.

Foxx grasped her hips and Maxine's lips sought his mouth. Her body writhed and she broke their kiss to throw back her head and cry out in ecstasy as she shuddered through a long, quivering orgasm.

Pulling her hips down, Foxx held her tightly until her last wave of shaking died away. Maxine let herself go limp, relaxing on Foxx's chest, her breast heaving. She lay on him quietly for several minutes, motionless, her head lolling on his shoulder.

Maxine lifted herself and looked at Foxx, then kissed him lightly. "I know we'll be more comfortable in bed. Isn't there a way for us to undress and get in bed without having to separate?"

"We'll never find that out unless we try," Foxx smiled.

"All I've got to do is let my robe slip off," Maxine said. "I don't know how you'd manage, though."

"Let's see if I can."

Foxx slid his hands into Maxine's armpits and lifted her as he rose from the chair. She let her robe slide to the floor and took off Foxx's shirt, then unbuttoned his undersuit. She tugged at his trousers and underwear, but her thighs were pressed so tightly around his hips that she could not get the garments off. Foxx started to pull away from her, but Maxine pressed herself to him even more firmly.

"No," she said. "It can't be done."

"Sure it can," Foxx told her. He lifted her again and took a long step that brought them to the side of the bed. "Lie down, now, and raise your legs up high." Maxine brought her legs up over his head, and Foxx grasped her hips. He swiveled her body until she faced the bed. "Now, kneel down," he told her. She did so, and Foxx's trousers and underwear slid down his legs into a heap on the floor.

"See? I told you we could do it," he said.

Foxx kicked his clothing out of the way and spread his feet wider on the floor. He grasped Maxine's hips in his hands and drove into her with a sudden lurch, then began stroking, withdrawing slowly until he almost left her, then thrusting hard until his hips met her upraised buttocks.

Maxine's body shook convulsively each time that Foxx drove in. Her muscles began contracting spasmodically after he'd made only a few deep thrusts, and instants later she began an orgasm that rose and faded a dozen times before she shook with a final wrenching climax.

Foxx drove even harder as he reached his own peak. He felt Maxine rising to a second tearing spasm, and held back until she entered it. Then he let himself go and spurted furiously, holding himself in her as he drained. Maxine's body sagged to the bed. Foxx released her hips then and lowered himself gently beside her, thoroughly spent.

CHAPTER 16

Foxx stirred restlessly and turned over. His outflung hand encountered warm, soft flesh. His touch roused Maxine but did not awaken her. Still asleep, she murmured something unintelligible, and her fingers brushed along his body briefly before she returned to her slumber. Feeling her caress brought Foxx partly awake, conscious enough to remember the long night, and how it had stretched until both he and Maxine had fallen into the deep sleep that follows satiety.

After his sleep had been disturbed, Foxx's mind began to function. Now he lay for a moment and looked up into the darkness of the shuttered room, wondering if a drink would put him back to sleep, knowing that a drink would mean a stogie, and knowing too that if he rose and moved around the room, he might waken Maxine. He closed his eyes, but sleep did not return.

Sighing silently, Foxx slipped from the bed and moved on bare feet to the table. He could see the room dimly in the hint of the night's starshine that trickled between the slats of the closed shutters. There was light enough for him to make out the bottle of Cyrus Noble, and to see the heap that his trousers and underwear made on the carpet beside the bed.

Foxx picked up the bottle and swallowed a satisfying draft of the smooth bourbon. His coat and vest hung over the back of the chair by which he stood. He took a stogie from the vest pocket, felt on the table until he found a match, and lit the stubby twisted cigar.

By the flare of the match he saw Maxine lying undisturbed, her skin warm cream on the white sheet. Her head was turned away from him. The vision of her innocent beauty, imprinted on Foxx's retinas by the match flare, persisted for several seconds while he slid his hand into the vest pocket holding his Pailliard hunting-case Repeater. He touched the chime lever, and the tiny tinkling that followed, muted by the fabric of the pocket, told him it was five o'clock.

Foxx had no idea what time he and Maxine had finally fallen asleep, but he was wide awake now. He sat down in the straight chair by the table and reached for the bottle of bourbon.

Before his lips touched the bottle's neck, a scraping sound from outside the window brought a frown to Foxx's face. Holding the bottle in midair, he fixed his eyes on the vague, dim horizontal pattern made by the shutter's louvers on the net curtain veiling the window inside the room.

For several moments he saw nothing; then the scraping noise sounded again. "Hell, it's more'n likely a mouse in the wall," Foxx muttered under his breath.

He sat without moving for a moment, not even lowering the bottle to the table. The scraping noise sounded again, and this time a quite audible tapping followed it.

Replacing the bottle of Noble on the table, Foxx picked up his Cloverleaf Colt and drew the hammer back to full cock. Foxx stood up and walked silently toward the window.

He had only two more short steps to take to reach the window when a sharp, clapping noise, two quick thuds like a hammer striking a board, sounded outside. Suddenly the faint light that had been seeping through the shutter slats was obscured. With the splintering sound of snapping wood and the high-pitched musical tinkle of breaking glass, the shutters gave way and the windowpane shattered. He heard Maxine utter a small surprised scream as she was roused by the noise.

Foxx half glimpsed the figure of a man behind the curtains as they bulged inward, and though he could not see the intruder's face through the fabric, he knew the man could only be Jed Morgan. Foxx brought up the Cloverleaf to fire, but Morgan's swinging entrance had already carried him across the short distance from the window. With a vicious kick Morgan knocked the pistol out of Foxx's hand before he could tighten his finger on the trigger.

Morgan's heavy boot landed a blow to Foxx's chest and sent him to the floor. While he was still falling, Foxx saw Morgan clawing for the heavy revolver that swung from his belt holster. Foxx hit the floor just as Morgan raised the pistol, and before his foe could fire, Foxx kicked upward. His foot was bare, but it hit Morgan's extended arm and sent the pistol flying across the room.

Foxx rolled to his feet, diving for Morgan with his arms spread to grasp the other man's body. Morgan leaped backward. His foot flew up, catching Foxx in the stomach. Foxx staggered back, gasping for breath. The rope on which Morgan had swung into the room was hanging in the broken-in window. Grabbing the rope, Morgan jumped. Foxx looked around for his Colt, but it had landed across the room by the door.

Crossing the room in three giant strides, Foxx picked up the Colt and ran back to the window. The rope holding Morgan was still swaying back and forth.

Foxx leaned out the window and looked down. Morgan had reached the ground now and was running down the street. He glanced over his shoulder as he ran, and even in the faint light of the starshine Foxx could recognize his hate-twisted face.

Foxx took a snap shot at the fleeing man, but Morgan was already beyond the range at which the stubby-barreled Cloverleaf was accurate. Morgan kept running toward the end of the street, turned right behind the last of Goldsburgh's houses, and disappeared.

"What—what was that?" Maxine gasped as Foxx pulled his head back into the room. She saw Foxx's face and asked quickly, "Oh, no! Not Jed Morgan?"

"It sure was." Foxx was untangling his underwear from his trousers. He slid into the linen undersuit and stepped quickly into the trousers.

"You're not going after him?"

"I can't let him get away this time, Maxine." Foxx looked at the window, a gray rectangle now clearly outlined, as he pushed his arms into his shirt sleeves. "Dawn's breaking. In a few minutes there'll be enough light to see by. And this time Morgan's running. He won't have time to cover his tracks."

"I'll go with you, Foxx," Maxine said, swinging her bare legs off the bed. "I've got my gun, and—"

"No!" Foxx told her firmly. "You'll stay right here with that gun in your hand. If Morgan shows up, use it!"

"You mean he might come back right away, so soon after—"

Foxx cut her question short. "Morgan's tricky. He could circle around and get back here before I catch up with him."

Maxine hesitated for a moment and then said reluctantly, "I guess you're right, Foxx. I'll stay here."

"Don't stay in this room—go next door to your own and keep the shutters latched. I don't think Morgan would try lowering a rope from the roof again, like he just done, but don't take a chance on it."

Foxx was forcing his bare feet into his heavy water buffalo-hide field boots. He strapped on the pistol belt that carried his Smith & Wesson in its cross-draw holster and reached for his coat. While he was checking his pockets to see that he had all he'd need, he said to Maxine, "Now, you do exactly what I told you to. I want you to promise me you will."

"All right, Foxx," Maxine said resignedly. "I promise."

"I'll be back as soon as I can. He ain't got too much of a start." Foxx started for the door, saw Maxine looking at him wistfully, and stopped by the bed to kiss her. "Now, don't worry. I'll be all right."

Apparently a stray shot on Goldsburgh's main street at dawn was not enough to arouse the curiosity of the town's residents. There was no one on the street, even though lights were beginning to glow in a few of the houses as Foxx walked rapidly through the silent town. He'd marked the place where Jed Morgan had turned, and stopped to search the ground beyond the street. By bending low and looking carefully, Foxx found the marks in the earth made by Morgan's boots.

Foxx followed the signs almost a quarter mile before he lost them at the point where Morgan had reached the trail. He searched along the rutted, hoof-pocked trail in both directions, but if the faint signs of the boot-scrapes were there, they were so intermingled with the deeper tracks of horse-hooves and wagon wheels that he could not see them.

Hunkering down beside the trail, Foxx reached into his vest pocket for a stogie and clamped it between his teeth. He reached for a match, but hesitated before striking it. Though the sky was now bright with the approaching sunrise, the flare would catch Morgan's attention at once if he was still near by. Then Foxx decided that it wasn't too likely the fugitive had stopped. Morgan had been moving in a straight line, an almost certain sign that he had some destination in mind.

Foxx lit the cigar, and by the time the stubby stogie had been reduced to a butt, Foxx had considered and discarded a half-dozen ideas. The one that had kept recurring to him would require time to execute, but it was the only one that seemed at all practical.

Fixing in his mind the unusually crooked branch in the top of a small scrub cedar that grew beside the trail, Foxx began to cast for tracks. He walked beside the trail for twenty paces, searching the ground carefully. Then he moved ten paces away from trailside and started back, angling toward the twisted cedar, still scanning the ground as he moved. Reaching the cedar, he reversed his course again after walking ten paces farther from the trail. For the next few minutes he moved back and forth, ten paces farther from the trail each time, until at last he saw the familiar boot-scrape, moving away from the trail.

With the direction in which Morgan was moving established by the angle of the scrape, Foxx had no trouble finding the next mark, and the next. Even though Morgan had stopped running soon after crossing the trail, he was moving across undisturbed ground now. Foxx found enough signs—a rock turned from the dimple in the ground where it had rested, the tip of a greasewood bush that had been ground into the earth by a bootheel, occasionally the print of the heel itself—to tell him where Morgan had passed.

Almost a mile from the trail the tumbledown surface buildings of an abandoned mine loomed ahead. Foxx followed Morgan's tracks over the heaped tailings. His foe's footprints were clear now in the softer soil that had been brought up from underground. Before he topped the shelter offered him by the last heap of tailings, Foxx stopped and took stock of his position.

Shading his eyes against the rising sun, he peered over the elongated pile of dirt and studied the high wooden walls of the hoist and the machine shed. They stood a little to one side of the massive square timbers that outlined the black opening of the main access tunnel. The roof of the tall, narrow building that once housed the hoisting gear had collapsed, and the building itself was beginning to sag. The machine shed was in better condition, its thick walls were sound, but the door and window casings yawned open; both windowpanes and door had long since been removed. Morgan's footprints led straight to the shed and disappeared inside it.

Foxx wasted no time, but took no foolish risks. He drew the Smith & Wesson and had it in his hand when he snaked over the top of the tailing heap. He was almost to the machine shed when the flicker of motion inside the building caught his eye. Foxx hit the ground, rolling toward the shed as a gun barked from its interior and a lead slug plowed into the ground where Foxx had hit before he'd started to roll.

Still in motion, Foxx fired. He aimed at the window where he'd seen the suggestion of someone moving. By the time Morgan got off a shot in reply, Foxx was past the window and the open door and had flattened himself against the wall of the shed.

"Morgan!" he called. "If you got any sense, you know you're cornered! I'll give you a chance to give up. Toss your gun out the window and walk out with your hands up!"

Foxx waited so long for a reply that he thought perhaps Morgan had ducked out of the back of the shed. When a reply to his offer finally came, it was a message of snarling defiance.

"Go to hell, Foxx! I'd be crazy to come out there where you can shoot me down! You'll have to come in after me!"

"I don't have to do a damn thing!" Foxx retorted. He tried a bluff. "You're the one that's pinned down. I can sit here until your throat gets so dry you'll be glad to come out!"

"It ain't any wetter out there than it is in here!" Morgan replied. "You'll dry up just as bad as I do while you're waiting for me to give in. Come on, Foxx! Come after me if you got the guts! I'm set and ready for you!"

Foxx knew his bluff had been called. He recognized the standoff they'd reached, and did not answer. Instead, he began cudgeling his brain for a way to get his quarry into the open. Inside the shed, he knew, Morgan was looking for his own solution—a way to escape.

To keep Morgan occupied, Foxx wasted a cartridge with a random shot into the doorway. He hadn't really expected Morgan to react, but an answering shot followed his, and a bullet whistled out the open space and kicked up dirt from the tailings.

Foxx opened the S&W and replaced the two cartridges he'd used, then with his free hand fished a stogie from his vest pocket and lit it. He blew out the match. For a moment he held the smoking matchstick in his fingers and looked at it. Then he let the match fall and took out his sheath-knife.

Working with his left hand, hugging the wall of the

shed in the narrow space between the door and window, Foxx began cutting at the doorframe. He brought the knife up at the edge of the wooden frame, twisting the blade to splinter the wood. He took his time, his ears alert for any sound of Morgan's movement. A few minutes of effort was all that he needed to filigree the edge of the dry wood of the doorframe into a line of wide splinters.

Inching to his left, Foxx worked on the outside edge of the windowframe as high up as he could reach. When he'd finished, he had a jagged line of tinder-dry splinters pulled free from the frame up one side of the window. Foxx surveyed his work, then took out a small sheaf of matches. He'd decided while he was working that Morgan would not respond to any threats he'd make. He struck one of the matches and held its flame under the bottom splinter. The thin, dry wood caught at once, and the flames ran quickly up the side of the frame. Swiveling around, Foxx struck a fresh match and lit the lowest splinter on the doorframe.

"Morgan!" he shouted. "You got no choice now! Come on out and give up! If you don't, you'll roast alive!"

There was no answer from inside the shed. Foxx waited until the flames at the window had spread over the entire side of the frame and were whipping inside before he risked looking into the shed. The slippery, crafty Morgan was not there. A hole in the roof at the back showed where he'd gotten out.

Foxx risked being shot from wherever Morgan had hidden. He ran around the corner of the shed. The cleared area around the buildings was empty. Foxx started for the rear of the little building, but stopped before he'd taken three steps. Morgan's boot-prints were clear on the bare soil. They led in a straight line to the yawning black entrance of the main access tunnel.

Unhesitatingly, Foxx followed the footprints. Blackness swallowed him before he'd gotten more than a few yards inside. He stepped back against the earthen wall and stopped to let his eyes adjust to the darkness. A shot broke the underground stillness, and a bullet shaved Foxx's ear as it thunked into the wall beside his head. Foxx dropped to the floor, his eyes trying to pierce the barrier of blackness, but could see only a few inches ahead along the floor of the tunnel.

"Morgan!" Foxx called. His voice reverberated and echoed in ghostly fashion in the blackness. "Now you really got yourself cornered! There's not any way you'll get outta here alive unless you give up!"

"Fuck you, Foxx!" Morgan's voice echoed in the same unearthly way that Foxx's had. "It's just as dark for you as it is for me! We're even, and I'll take my chances on even odds! If you want me, come and get me!"

Foxx took up the challenge. He began belly-crawling along the tunnel floor. Ahead he could hear the faint sounds of Morgan's retreating footsteps. The floor of the tunnel had been beaten smooth by the booted feet of the miners who'd trodden it over the years, and he could make fast progress. Once, he stopped long enough to look back. The mouth of the tunnel seemed to have shrunk in size; it showed now as a square of light no bigger than a man's handkerchief.

Suddenly Foxx realized that he could no longer hear Morgan moving ahead of him. He stopped to listen. There was no sound of movement from the darkness ahead.

For a moment Foxx could not decide whether to shout or shoot. Morgan made up his mind for him.

Muzzle flashes from Morgan's pistol lit up the blackness of the tunnel. Their brilliance blinded Foxx in the instant before he closed his eyes and rolled against the tunnel wall while lead flew above him and thudded into the earthen sides of the mine shaft.

Morgan kept firing until he'd emptied his revolver. Foxx had not really seen his quarry before closing his eyes, but he returned Morgan's fire now, three shots that he spaced across the width of the tunnel as best he could by guess, for the blackness into which he was shooting was impenetrable. The flare of his own revolver's muzzle showed him Morgan, kneeling on the floor, reloading.

Foxx's S&W still held the two cartridges he'd reserved. He used them now, aiming by memory, rolling across to the opposite side of the tunnel as soon as he'd triggered the gun twice. The second shot drew a yelp of pain from the darkness, then Morgan had his own pistol reloaded. He peppered the spot where Foxx had been lying, but none of the slugs that buried themselves in the dirt came near their intended target.

Foxx dug into his pocket for more shells. His hand encountered the cartridge cases he'd made into miniature flares in anticipation of the raid on the outlaws in the coulee.

"I got him now," Foxx muttered to himself. There was no note of triumph in his tone, only the grim finality that marked the beginning of the end of an unpleasant job.

Before taking out the flares, Foxx reloaded the S&W. He kept it in his hand despite the handicap it gave him of being forced to work with his left hand in taking the flares out of his pocket and lining them up on the earth floor beside him. Foxx worked with careful urgency. He had no way of knowing whether Morgan was holding the position where he'd been when Foxx had seen him last or whether his foe was advancing after being wounded.

With the flares lined up where he could grab them without fumbling, Foxx made one last try. He called, "You're hurt now, Morgan! Give up while you still got time! I won't waste no more breath asking you! This is the last chance you'll get!"

"I make my own chances, Foxx!" Morgan shouted back. "If you think you're good enough, come on and take me!"

Foxx picked up the flares and lined them up in his left hand. He bent his knee to bring his foot within reach and drew the matchstick head of the first flare across his bootsole. The match sputtered alight. Foxx tossed the flare as far as he could down the tunnel, then in quick succession lit and threw two more.

When the first match flamed up, Morgan fired, but in the total darkness the moving light of the matchhead was enough to blind him and spoil his aim. He rose to his feet, staggering, and let off another shot just as the tunnel was suddenly bathed in brilliant light.

Foxx was prepared. He had Morgan in his sights as the outlaw rose, and his first shot went home. Morgan was falling as Foxx triggered his second shot, and its bullet buried itself in the tunnel's wall.

In the sudden light Foxx could see why Morgan had not been able to go deeper into the mine. He was standing at the edge of the vertical shaft through which the hoist had once run.

As Foxx watched his foe crumpling, Morgan raised his revolver in a last desperate effort. His unsteady hand triggered the weapon before he leveled it, but Foxx had fired again at the beginning of Morgan's move. The simultaneous reports brought clods of dirt down from the roof of the tunnel at the edge of the shaft.

Morgan fired again, a dying reflex that sent a bullet harmlessly into the tunnel floor. The flares still illuminated the tunnel. Foxx saw the edges of the shaft crumbling. A crack opened in the tunnel roof ten feet from the shaft and in a fraction of a second widened as a mass of earth at the end of the roof began sliding down.

Just as the last flare sputtered out Foxx saw the falling earth engulf Morgan and carry him into the open shaft.

There were several more of the miniature flares in Foxx's pocket. He lit one and tossed it down the tunnel, then by its light walked down to the edge of the shaft. Foxx did not know whether his shot had killed Morgan or whether the massive heap of dirt under which his foe now lay had smothered him. He stood for a moment gazing at the bottomless darkness that would be Morgan's unmarked grave. Then he holstered his S&W and walked slowly toward the small square of daylight that gleamed at the mouth of the tunnel.

DELL'S ACTION-PACKED WESTERNS

Selected Titles